NICHOLAS KNIGHT'S

NIGHTSHADE

BOOK 2

DARK
FUGITIVE

The Nightshade Series, Book 2

NICHOLAS KNIGHT

Burning Bulb

PUBLISHING

Dark Fugitive
By **Nicholas Knight**
Burning Bulb Publishing
P.O. Box 4721
Bridgeport, WV 26330-4721
United States of America
www.BurningBulbPublishing.com

Cover designed by Natasa Ilincic.

First Edition.
Paperback Edition ISBN: 978-0-9977730-5-7

Printed in the United States of America

PREFACE

DAWN'S TALE (Book 1) introduces us to Dawn Moon, a sexy, 18-year-old Cherokee, who finds herself in a Virginian psychiatric facility in 1977. She is soon joined by new patient, Reuben Ian Peterson, an older, less attractive man, whom she is immediately smitten with. These two broken souls fall passionately in love, which is the last thing that Nurse Carl wants to see happen. Carl is a sadistic bully, who is obsessed with Dawn and wants her for his own. This fairy tale is cut short and Reuben is taken away too soon, the moment Nurse Carl's selfish jealousy gets the best of him. When this perverted sociopath loses his temper and drives a makeshift stake through Reuben's heart, Dawn snaps, and sets off on a violent adventure that she can never recover from.

DEDICATIONS

For Erica Linnette Heath: You were, are, and always will be the love of my life and afterlife. I miss you so much, baby. Everything I do, everything I am, is for you and my beloved daughter. Thank you for forgiving me, for still loving me, and for giving me hope that we will be together in Heaven someday. Thank you for loving and watching over our little girl. You would have made a wonderful Mommy, and as far as I'm concerned, you *are* Harley's mother. I promise you, that the next time I get to hold you, I will never let go. Thank you for being my creative consultant on parts of this novel, for sharing and suggesting your ideas, and for once again bringing light to my otherwise dark world. I look forward to being your forever partner in the sky, and eternally having you in my arms again. I love you, Erica, with all my heart and soul. I love you to the moon and back. I will never give up on or abandon you, and I will never lose hope that God will let us be reunited in Paradise. Time will never change our love, and nobody will ever come between us. Thank you for still wanting me, and for gracing me with this second chance. I will always defend your honor against the bullies and charlatans of this world. You're the only one who ever made love to me, instead of using my love against me. Nobody will ever compete with or replace you, nor would I want them to. You and Harley are everything to me, Erica. The word, *love,* does not nearly describe or express how I feel for you, or what you mean to me. Love is just not a big enough word. Clergymen like to preach that none of us are perfect, but they didn't know you. Thank you, Erica, for your pure heart and your perfect love. You and Harley give my life meaning. (February 22, 1980 - December 27, 2002)

For Harley Linnette Delorie: I am so proud to be your father, Harley, and only wish I could have provided better for you, had the honor of raising you, or at the very least chosen a woman who could have loved us back. Erica should have been your Mommy, and in many ways…is. I'm sorry, sweetheart, that the world is so cold and that life has treated us both so badly. You are the daughter I have always wanted and so much more, and (much like my love for Erica) I will never give up on you or quit loving you. There is nothing you could ever do to lose me, honey. I'm sorry that I wasn't able to be a bigger part of your life, Harley. God knows I wanted to be. There is not a moment or day that goes by, where I don't think of you, worry about you, miss you, or wonder how you're doing or what is happening in your life. I'm sorry that I couldn't be a better man, or make better choices, or have any success in life. Just know that no other man could have loved you more deeply, or been happier to be your father. Even long after I'm gone, Erica and I will both be watching over you, worrying about, and praying for you. I love you, *Harley girl*.

For Russell Clayton Harris, Jr: My kind Uncle whom I have forever felt a strong connection with. Though you were taken far too soon, and I was very young when you passed, I have always known we were kindred spirits. Who knew we would be so alike, and lead such parallel lives? You were never just an extended relative to me, but a close friend. Thank you, Uncle Russ, for being such a genuine and gentle soul, in spite the horrible hand you were tragically dealt. I am so very sorry for the pain you endured in this world, and wish that there was something I could do to make things right or bring justice to those who took you from us. I love you as much as one man can love another man without being gay. I trust that God will see in you what Jen and I do. I hope to see you in paradise, assuming that God welcomes us both into Heaven, which I pray He will. (March 31, 1952 - November 22, 1982)

For Natasa Ilincic: Thank you so much for contributing your time and your inspiring talent to this book cover. When I was younger, I was often told that I was an exceptional artist, but my ability has never come close to matching yours. You are a phenomenal artist, and I am grateful to have the honor of having your enchanting work on the cover of this first sequel. Thank you so much for illustrating such magic, and helping me further bring these characters to life. You rock, Natasa! Thank you for sharing your gift. I appreciate your talent and your friendship.

For Gary Lee Vincent: Thank you for believing in me and this trilogy. I will never forget what you've done for me and my fictional daughter, *Dawn*. You are a good man and a good friend. Thank you, Gary. You have my eternal gratitude.

For Tiger: You are my spirit animal, and an invaluable and irreplaceable friend. Thank you for being so attentive, and so unbelievably caring. You're a wonderful companion. Thank you for keeping me company while I wrote this book, and for keeping me alert and motivated. Erica knew what she was doing when she brought us together. She knew we needed each other. She's so much smarter than I ever knew, and certainly far brighter than myself. Thank you, Erica, for *Tiger*. Thank you for everything. We both love you very much.

For Jen Bartlebaugh: Thank you for being the longest friendship I've ever had. Thank you for collaborating your creative input and advice to this second story. This novel would not be what it is without you and Erica. Thanks, Jen.

For Jennifer Lee Hassel: It hurt to lose you to Chris, back in January of 1992, but you would prove to be the only ex-lover I would ever know, who would later apologize to me and forgive me. That may seem small to some, but not to me. Thank you, Jennifer, for being different. I'm sorry that we can't be in each other's lives, but I'm grateful to know that you and I are okay again. You will always have a place in my heart, Jennifer, even if you never wanted me like I wanted you. I wish you only the best in life, and am glad I got to know you, even if only for a brief pause.

My future may get bleaker by the hour, but I hope that these books I've written may contribute to my legacy. I'm very proud of this trilogy, and I know that those who read it will fall in love with *Dawn*, as I have.

WOLF PRAYER

Spirit of the Wolf
You who wanders the wild lands
You who stalks in silent shadows
You who runs and leaps
Between the moss covered trees
Lend me your primal strength
And the wisdom of your glowing eyes
Teach me to relentlessly track my desires
And to stand in defense of those I love
Show me the hidden paths and moonlit fields
Fierce spirit
Walk with me in my solitude
Howl with me in my joy
Guard me as I move through this world

- Travis Bowman

3500-4000 BC
OMINOUS GENESIS

The Christian Bible, when truly analyzed and evaluated, often contradicts itself in many places. This especially happens with the overabundance of alleged *translations*, which is the obnoxious result of everyone wanting to incorporate their own opinions and interpretations into a doctrine, which was intended to be held sacred and unaltered. (Rev. 22:18-19). This makes it very confusing, and impossible, to know what is accurate and what is sabotaged, because of the growing various versions of the Gospel, which continue to consistently accumulate and increase over time.

Isaiah 34:14 is a prime example of this literary and chaotic nightmare. Depending on which alleged translation you choose to reference, or invest your faith in, you usually get an entirely different reading of this same verse.

The Bible also tells us that it's offensive to God when we look upon someone with lust, and yet God was the one who designed our bodies to be the way they are. In fact, according to the Book of Genesis, God asked Adam and Eve why they were ashamed of their nudity, after they disobeyed him. Yet, modern-day *Christians* will look down on you, if you look at a nude photograph or watch a *dirty* movie.

In the *New International Version* (or NIV), it says in Genesis 1:26 that God said, *let us make mankind in our image and in our likeness, so that they can rule over all the creatures of the land, sea, and air*. Notice that the verse says, *in our image* and *in our likeness*. Is this a flawed oversight in this translation, further proving the legitimate argument that there are entirely too many versions of the written Gospel? Or, did God really intend to use the words *us* and *our* instead of *my*?

It is widely believed in both Judaism and Satanism, that these questionable Scripture verses were the direct result of there being two variants of the Creation story, the former of which was discarded and unused. The accepted explanation for this, is that Adam had a wife before Eve, and that she was a disappointment to Adam and an abomination unto the Creator. Her name was *Lilith* (which is the Hebrew word for, *of the night*). The legend goes that Lilith had a hostile argument with Adam, about his wishes for her to be submissive to him sexually. She callously abandons Adam, refusing to be subservient or faithful, and flagrantly rebels against God by hooking up with the serpent-like archangel, Samael, and whoring herself instead to him. The brazenly selfish Lilith is then ousted from the Garden of Eden, and is justly forsaken and banished by God.

After God cast her out of the Garden, three angels chased after Lilith to try and persuade her to come back, but they found Lilith at the Red Sea, where she vowed to take her retribution against Jehovah, by feasting on human infants. God puts a spell over Adam, causing him to slip into a comatose state, where he then uses one of Adam's ribs to create a more pleasing and suitable companion. Lilith later bears demonic offspring from her obscene union with the dark angel, which some would argue is where we get the nephilim from, who are briefly mentioned in Genesis 6:4. Others would say that this is where we get the *evil beasts* in 2 Peter 2:12, Titus 1:12, Leviticus 26:6, and Ezekiel 5:17. The Bible also makes a point to talk about the world falling into darkness, and the moon being covered in blood (Acts 2:20 and Joel 2:31). The Christian Gospel also forbids us to drink the blood of any living being (Leviticus 17:14 and Deuteronomy 12:23).

It is said that Lilith eventually crossed paths with the homicidal Cain, in the wastelands where she had settled. They engaged in violent sex, and then she taught him the power of drinking blood and binging on human flesh. Since Lilith had not partaken of the forbidden fruit from the Tree of Life, the way that Adam and Eve did, many believe that she was never subject to sickness or death. Some, in the modern Christian community, would be quick to doubt that God could mistakenly make such a heinous succubus, but these same people tend to forget that God also created Lucifer. Eve would, of course, betray Adam as well, as would many wives for the endless centuries and generations to come.

When Eve bites into the crisp apple, it's after Samael deludes her into believing that it will improve and intensify her lovemaking with Adam, as she had been secretly disappointed and unsatisfied with the size of his pink torpedo.

"The blossoms of the tree will bring love, romance, and seduction, in ways you can't begin to imagine," he told her. "God forbids this delicious fruit, because he wants to deprive you of the euphoric delights you deserve. He wants to deny you the hedonistic inhibitions that you naturally crave. God gave you these desires, so they can't be bad. God put this tree here to tease you, because he's cruel and sadistic. Don't let him keep you from what is rightfully yours," the serpent-like angel hissed, cunningly in her ear.

"But, my Adam will be peeved," she told the deceptive viper, with feigned concern for Adam's feelings, purely for the sake of appearance and arrogance.

"Adam is out romping with the animals. He should be enrapturing your luscious figure, not naming those with four legs. You don't require his permission, Eve. Take what belongs to you," the vile incubus told her.

As the ignoble and scaled minion tightly embraced her from behind, and reached around to cup her milky breast with his taloned hand, she found herself speaking words that were foreign to her, in ways which were deplorable and dishonorable. She began to speak in this strange tongue, as if being telepathically inspired and influenced by the slithering and slimy, Samael.

"Spirit of this blossomed tree, open up our eyes and make us see. Work your magick through our veins, until no trace of God remains. This, I pray, to this forbidden tree. Guide us now, so mote it be," she prayed, thereby becoming the first witch of the oldest religion.

As Eve placed her soft lips up against the damned fruit, she further proves that she, much like Lilith, is only warm on the outside.

Samael chimes in, and recites a different ghastly chant, as he relishes in watching Eve bite into the tantalizing apple. "Fruit of death, fruit of life, fruit of the spirit, fruit that eases mortal strife. Ease the hunger of the undead, until they reach their final stead. Be food enough for everyone, until their journey is pure poison."

God saw this abomination, and watched Eve infect Adam, as she spread her betrayal and blasphemy like wildfire. Jehovah gave them both a chance to confess their sin, only to be met with duplicity. Jehovah, in his supreme anger, threw down a bolt of lightning. Adam and Eve were able to dodge the rod, but it struck the apple, slicing it crosswise. After they had scattered and sheltered for a time, they returned to where the apple laid and picked it up. Holding the four quarters together, they saw that the seeds and core made a perfect pentagram. God was, of course, still watching them.

God turned his back to them and threw them away, as so many Christians would later be known to do to others, and as so many women would later come to do to the men they gave empty intimacy and simulated commitment. God placed a cherubim at the entrance to the Garden, to prevent Adam and Eve from re-entering the earthly paradise. The cherubim was covered with eyes from head to toe, had six wings, and was as terrifying as any demon that hovered over the river Styx. Eve would bear and rear Adam's children, but she would never genuinely love him, which would set a cruel and callous trend for the rest of time.

It is written, that Adam would eventually fall into the pool of vanity, upon seeing his mirrored reflection on the surface of the water. This in turn, combined with enduring such brutal mistreatment from Lilith and Eve, would be the birth of misogyny, and make Adam the first male narcissist and original homosexual. Others believe that this was the direct result of him being forced to accept the agonizing reality that he would never know true love, or find a good heart, at least not from the opposite sex.

APPROX 2200 BC
THE BIRTH OF ISIS

Nimrod developed the concept behind astrology, laying the foundation for both white and black witchcraft. He was the builder of Babylon, and the High Priest of a Pagan grotto that worshipped the moon and sacrificed babies. The group was designed to be a blatant blasphemy against the Christian God, Jehovah. Nimrod's basic message was that our flesh is beautiful, not sinful, and that we have no need for a Savior. Nimrod's great Uncle, Shem (one of Noah's three sons), became so outraged, that he not only murdered Nimrod in cold blood, but decapitated him and dismembered his body.

Nimrod's whorish mother, Semiramis, led the Occultic group into becoming subterranean. It was while hiding underground that she announced that her executed son (who was also her incestuous lover), had actually been a deity. This, in turn, made her a goddess. Even though Nimrod had clearly been mortal, and never rose from the grave, Semiramis was successful in brainwashing the coven into buying her batshit story. This would go down in history as being the first cult, where the leader's charisma and charm would override any intelligence and education with crackpot theories and blind indoctrination.

Semiramis arrogated the title, *The Queen of Heaven*, and later became better known as *Isis*. She was identified by a symbol, which was a crescent moon accompanied by a small black five-pointed star. She was quickly and majorly worshipped throughout Egypt. She convinced her gluttony of followers that she was a virgin, and that her sons had all been immaculate conceptions.

Isis bore a second son, whom she named Tammuz. She claimed that Tammuz was Nimrod reincarnated. Tammuz eventually became known as, Baal, the Sun God. When Babylon fell, Baal's and Isis' approval rating only skyrocketed, and they became more venerated and exalted than ever.

Shem's other great nephew, Cush, was one of Isis' polygamous husbands. Cush was also Nimrod's father (1 Chronicles 1:10) and Noah's grandson. He was Isis' third son, and would be the infamous architect of the Tower of Babel.

Nimrod was also known as *Osiris*, and Baal was also known as the aliases, *Sol*, and *Horus*. Much like Satan, these three people went by several different identities.

Isis' symbol would later be adopted by another hateful pedophile named, Muhammad, who would found, and establish, the radically wicked religion of Islam.

JULY 3, 1971
THE WORT MOON

Pamela Courson walks into the luxury bathroom of their glamorous *La Marais* residence, and finds her rock-idol boyfriend stone cold in the Parisian tub, after deliberately tricking him into believing that heroine was cocaine. Jim avoided heroine like the plague, just like Ritchie Valens avoided flying for most of his life. Pamela shook him violently, in desperate attempt to revive him, but Jim wouldn't wake up...he was gone, at 27. Pam would later join her *cosmic mate* three years later, from a heroin overdose, also dying tragically at 27. Meanwhile, Linda Moon is having her own ill-fated adventure, but in the sandy outskirts of Egypt.

Linda had gone on a missions trip with the Nazarene church, to Cairo. There, she visited one of the pyramids at Giza, where there were mummified bodies buried in ancient tombs, underneath the grotesquely greedy and covetously sovereign. She sees hieroglyphics, on the walls, of primordial etchings and engravings of exalted creatures that have wolf heads on human bodies. These represented demiurge beasts who adored and adulated throughout Egypt, since 600 BC. She is sporting sunglasses that have forest-green frames and pumpkin-tinted lenses. Linda's wandering eye catches sight of a Middle-Eastern man whom she finds to be tall, dark, and handsome. She immediately notices his wedding ring, but decides to hit on him anyway.

"Hi," Linda says, with a coquettish smile, to break the ice. "What's your sign, hot stuff?"

The man she had approached was dressed in a spirited, skinny rib turtleneck, distinctively and fashionably belted. It had hemmed, long sleeve cuffs and bottom. The guy wore Perma-Press herringbone, stripe flared jeans. They were low rise, and rode on the hip bone with a snug fit that followed the contours of his body. He wore a lapel pin on the upper left side of his turtleneck, in the shape of an Ankh, which pridefully indicated his affiliation with the Islamic faith. His footwear were nostalgic *Gucci* 1953, horsebit crocodile loafers, which matched the shade of his Hunter Green turtleneck. He had perfect posture, and was clean cut. To look at this upscale snob, it was pretty obvious that he was swimming in wealth, which only managed to heighten Linda's debased interest.

"I'm flattered," he said in response, "but I'm married."

"I can dig it," she replied without hesitation, showing her gross lack of character, "So am I. But, hey, what they don't know won't hurt 'em, right?" she said, audaciously and shamelessly, grabbing his crotch over his pants and tenderly beginning to massage it.

The corporate CEO quickly pushed her hand away from his semi-erect groin, and yelled at her, making even more of a scene. Linda reeked of pot, leaving no doubt that she had been toking grass. Truth was, he found her exceptionally arousing, but he couldn't afford to let that be known, so he did his best to play it off, as if her very existence and presence insulted and offended him.

"That will be enough, harlot!" he shouted crossly. "Have you no respect for my faith?! If you were in my land, you would be beheaded for your brass promiscuity!" Leaving her there to wallow in the humiliation that she was incapable of feeling, he heatedly stomped off in a tantrum.

An unassociated Sufi woman sees this happen and steps up to Linda, proffering her a small stone from inside her black, woolen Burka, which Linda doesn't know is cursed. The Muslim, of course, doesn't let on that she has cruel intentions, but appears to simply be rendering a friendly gesture. The peculiar woman's hand looks to be young, on the surface. Linda is hesitant to trust the Islamic stranger, but doesn't wish to affront her foreign culture, so she humbly accepts what she mistakes as a gracious gift.

"Thank you. What's your name, doll?" Linda asks, as she willingly takes the stone into her left hand, noticing that it bore a strange hieroglyphic in its center.

"Lilith," the woman answers, "and you're most welcome." As Lilith speaks, Linda can hear a legion of different and distinct voices flowing from her hidden mouth.

Before Linda could fully grasp what was happening, she felt a sudden burning sensation in her hand. She immediately tried to drop the stone, but couldn't get rid of it, as it had magically attached itself to her mortal flesh. As Linda watches in horror, the stone sears into her naked palm, leaving her with a permanent branding of the primeval symbol that was carved into it. The mystical stone, itself, had vanished without a trace, leaving no evidence or ash. The pagan marking, scorched on Linda's palm, was an inverted cross with a crescent moon resting atop.

Linda suddenly discovers that she possesses the power to see things that others cannot. Though Lilith remains draped in the concealing burka, Linda can see her as she truly is. For the most part, Lilith appears to be a normal Arabic woman, but has abnormally large and circular eyes, which bare no pupils, but rather solid onyx. Her hair is interminable, bristly, and charcoal. To everyone else in that room, Lilith was still cloaked in her coffin-like, Islamic garb. Linda, however, now saw right through the demon.

"What are you?" Linda asked, under her breath, as she could feel her skin begin to crawl and tremor in undefinable, petrifying fear.

Linda fiddled with the bow that was tied around her waist, while Lilith gave her a creepy cheshire grin, which unveiled her yellowed fangs that looked inhuman and malformed. Linda stares for another split second, into her dark eyes, and then runs to the nearest trash receptacle, and vomits. When she turns back to again look at Lilith, her sinister adversary had strangely evanesced from sight. There was a black cloud of thick smoke in the shape of an owl where Lilith had stood, leaving behind a suffocating odor of sulfur and brimstone.

The slutty preacher's wife had partaken in this missions trip, with the admirable ambition to fight the disease of Islam, which continued to rapidly spread its infection. She had no reason to foresee this honorable effort backfiring, and coming back to bite her in the ass. When Linda leaves the *Pyramid of Khufu*, she feels terribly feeble and frail. She suckered herself into believing the whopper that it was nothing more than food poisoning, having no clue what vicious hex Lilith had placed on not only her, but also on those she was related to by blood.

NOVEMBER 1, 1977
FOG MOON

The numerous motorists continued to pass her by without glance or gesture, despite the fact that a law officer now laid and bled on the asphalt, in plain daylight. Dawn got out of her stolen *Chevy* wagon and carefully lifted, dragged, and positioned the traffic cop against the side of his cruiser. Luckily, he had left the keys in the vehicle and the doors unlocked, which made it all the easier to pop the trunk. She sifted and searched until she found a German-made, steel, 26.5mm flare pistol. She took this gun in her hand, left the trunk exposed, and pulled open the little door to the fuel filler cap. After twisting off the cap, she took several steps back into the open highway, while there was a significant break in traffic.

From out of nowhere, a silver Lotus *Esprit M70* materialized only feet from Dawn, nearly hitting her. She instinctively jumped into the air, literally vaulting over the mechanical speedster. As Dawn landed safely and miraculously on all fours, she abruptly stood up and turned around to look at the motorized bullet she had dodged. As the European hotrod got smaller and more distant, Dawn's sharp sight was at least able to make out the license plate. It was a vanity tag, which read *SIX-6-SIX*.

Aiming the best she could, the inexperienced Dawn shot a road flare at the open gas tank. Those drivers who were currently on the freeway, honked and cursed at her, sticking their heads out to give her the bird, as they lividly swerved around her. With the help of beginner's luck, the flare went in without problems, causing the police car to explode and launch like a rocket. The impact of the blast blew Dawn back, and landed her back first on the front windshield of a moving car.

"Jesus Christ!" the driver yelled, as Dawn's body considerably cracked his windshield and led him to lose visual of the stretch of road before him, as well as handling the traction of his wheels.

As the driver panicked and fishtailed in the middle of the highway, cars did their best to brake completely or move out of his way, to avoid crashing or being part of a pileup. In the midst of all this mayhem, Dawn was thrown off the spacious hood, after failing to hold on to the substantial vehicle. As soon as she flew off the 1977 *Lincoln Continental*, and into the woods, an eighteen-wheeler rammed the damaged car, instantly killing the newlywed couple who were its contents.

This time, people did acknowledge and act, as several drivers pulled over or ran off road. Many got out of their vehicles and searched for the female menace; but Dawn was already gone. She had wasted no time in picking herself up and dusting herself off, to begin fleeing from the scene. As she ran, she did so with such speed and force, that her knees poked through her *Jordache* bellbottoms. She stopped, just long enough to rip her hiphuggers into denim cut-offs, and resumed to sprinting and leaping through the trees, leaving the *Chevy* wagon and the calamity behind her. She would have preferred to be wearing a pair of nylon running shorts, but her claws were sufficient in customizing her hiphuggers into *Daisy Dukes*. This time was also different, in that people took notice of what she looked like, and in return, would let others know what they saw. One guy actually stopped and promised to backtrack a couple miles, where he recalled spotting a payphone, so he could notify the police of this automotive catastrophe.

Dawn was wounded, but was pleasantly shocked to find that her injuries were minor. She had a few cuts and scrapes, but that was about the extent of it. She had fortunately thought enough to pocket the money she had found in the hippy family's wagon, before leaving it behind with the rest of the devastation and havoc she had created. Dawn sprinted, as if urgently racing against time, carrying herself effortlessly on all fours while she once again fled from accountability.

Dawn eventually makes it back to Washington National Pike North, after exhausting herself from relying on her own hands and feet. She had gone as far as she could on her own merit, but was now running on empty. Dawn was special, but far from immortal. Her aptitude for the paranormal only lasted so long, before it gave out. Once she had made her way back to the road, she was able to hail a taxi, which was all too happy to help her out. She noticed the *Virginia is for Lovers* phrase on the vanity plate of the cab, which left a bitter taste in her mouth, and just reminded her of how cruel and unjust God is. The black sheep could feel herself lose her mind. She had been crazy about Reuben, which was why she was now going crazy without him.

"Where you headed, momma?" the driver asked, who was of African race, and had a crazed afro hairstyle.

"I don't care," she said. "Just drive."

"I understand, little minx, but I need to know where to take you," he insisted.

"I'm having a rough day," she said. "Please, just drive," she stressed, making every effort to remain polite and not blow this ride.

"Okay," he agreed. "You can pay me, right? When we stop, I need you to honor what the meter says," he subtly warned, while ogling at her body in the rearview mirror, squinting to try and see through her creamy, poet-sleeved blouse.

"That's fine," she yielded. "I'll pay the fare, whatever it is," she said, as she laid back and placed her hand over her eyes, as if to use her palm as a padded sleep mask. "Just keep going West, away from fucking Virginia."

"Dig it," he replied, causing Dawn to roll her eyes in disgust, as that particular word had become a personal pet peeve.

While Dawn was progressively passing out and working toward catching up on some much-needed rest, she hears the chorus to The Raiders' 1971 released billboard hit, *Indian Reservation*, on the car stereo. The over-zealous chauffeur got her back on Interstate 270 North, which in turn, put her back on track. They soon hit I-70W, near Hagerstown, which is where they cross into Pennsylvania. He eventually reaches Interstate 76, and takes her into Pittsburgh. The ride in the yellow cab was fairly peaceful, since the automotive pilot seemed to mind his own business and not make small talk. However, he would change his tune at the end of the line.

Dawn was revived, to find the cabbie vigorously shaking her left arm with his left hand, as he hovered over top of her, in the back seat. He had parked the car in an underground lot, somewhere in the business district of Steel City.

"Hey," he said. "Look around you, look up here. Take time to make time, make time to pay the fucking fare!"

Dawn yawned, then stretched her legs and arms, just to realize that he was practically laying on top of her. Luckily, his trousers were on and he was holding himself up with his double-jointed elbows. He was a smooth operator, and knew exactly what he was doing. He had her right where he wanted her, or so he thought. Dawn noticed that he had a young blonde sitting in the front passenger seat, who spun around to mirthfully watch his rape endeavor.

"C'mon, Marianne," the driver persisted, "This ain't no midnight train to Georgia. I've taken you far enough, without payment. It's time to dance for me. It's time to pay the fucking fiddler," he said, still jolting her until he could verify that she was up and alert.

"Where are we?" Dawn asked, suffering from a pulsating migraine, and deaf to him calling her by another name. "Fuck my head," she said, holding the sides of her skull as if afraid it would fall off, not caring or realizing whom she was dialoguing with.

"I took you to Pittsburgh, sweet thang," he answered her. "You made it as far as Pennsylvania, baby. I need two grand from you," he ordered, outrageously over-charging, while taking her for a fool who could be easily duped.

"Two grand?" she asked, in a delirious frenzy. "As in two thousand dollars?"

"That's right, momma," he decreed, eager to swindle her and take advantage of what he mistook to be green virtue. "That's what the meter says, baby, and the meter don't lie."

"Are you fucking me?" she asked inadvertently, with a Freudian slip. "You must be tripping. I didn't just fall off the goddamn money tree. I can't pay that," she explained, not that she had ever intended on giving him what was due, anyway.

"Yeah, I figured as much," he admitted, not the least bit surprised. "I swear, if I had a dime for every honky-jive customer who took me for a ride, when I should be the one enjoying that role...I'd be a wealthy mother fucker."

"Why are you smiling?" she asked, seeing the shit-eating grin plastered on his face, as if he was up to no good.

"Oh, baby," he began again, "you're a gas. You're going to pay me, bitch. You just don't know it yet."

"I told you," she said, now getting turbulent with him, "I don't fucking have that kind of dough! Are you a zombie? Are you brain-dead? I can't pay you what I can't afford!"

That unsettling chill returned without warning, and once again had nothing to do with Dawn being cold. This time though, it revealed itself as more than just an invisible presence. Dawn could now see what had begun to haunt her. It was a specter, that appeared to be seated in the driver's seat, though she was the only one who could see it. This apparition spooked Dawn, as it was vivid but translucent. It was blueish in tinge, and was in the shape of a naked woman. The phantom was hunched over with her back turned to Dawn. It also seemed to be holding its ears and ululating placidly. Dawn's skin was shrouded in goose bumps, though the sleazy hired hand would fail to notice.

"There are alternative ways to compensate me for the ride, sugar," he said, as restitution…in the form of sexual favors…had been his hidden intention all along. "You be trippin' if you believe I'm gonna enable a freeloader. Oh yeah, you gonna put on a show. You gonna pay me what I want, bitch."

"Hey, no offense," she told him as nicely as possible, "but I'm just not interested. Why don't you take your ridiculous fee out of that bimbo?" she suggested, referring to the incontestable slut who was getting her debauched kicks from her impromptu and unscrupulous spectating.

Dawn tried to break away by squirming out from under him, when he lost his temper. He grabbed her by the shoulders and slammed her back down.

"Look, dime-store bitch," he said, not as endearing this time. "I'm all about free love, but you're waging war with me now. I don't give to charity, mama. I gave you a slow ride, so now you gonna reward the favor," he said, grabbing her boob and squeezing it roughly, as if trying to juice a ripe melon.

Dawn looked at his hand clutching her breast, and then sneered up at him.

"What's with the simper fi? Why you crackin' that smile, hoochie mama?" he asked aggressively, while reaching down with his free hand, and unbuckling his pants. "This brutha's gonna make you squeal," he threatened, referring to himself in the third person.

"Can't you just hold me? Please?" she asked, with a puppy-dog meme, as she batted her eyes, and covered her upper lip with her lower one. "I'm so lonely," she divulged.

The lust-induced chauffeur fell for her counterfeit whim, while letting his boner wave like a pendulum, as if it used its own mind to seek a warm sheath. He slid his right hand down her soft torso and grabbed hold of her waistband, as if planning to rip her altered jeans clear off her foxy form.

"Please," she begged again, "I'll submit to doing whatever you tell me. I'll grant your every heart's desire. Just please...hold me first. I just want you to hug me for a moment, so I can at least pretend that you care for me."

Though tender affection wasn't his typical *modus operandi*, he couldn't argue that her entreaty was a reasonable trade for what he would take in exchange.

"That's not my bag, momma," he avowed, "but it's a fair request. Since you asked so nicely, come here," he ordered her, while leaning down and nuzzling his face against hers, as he canoodled her with phony benevolence.

"Bad move," she whispered exclusively in his ear, as he caressed her neck with his revolting tongue. Before he knew it, she had wrapped her arms around him and secured him in a headlock. "Now, it's my turn," she said, smiling back, but with a whole different meaning behind it and without him seeing it.

Dawn heard the drumming again, in the sound of hoofbeats and in the tempo of galloping hooves. The wraith suddenly turned around and wailed loudly at Dawn, just before her wayward daughter killed the scheming deviant. Dawn flicked out her middle finger and jabbed it into the cabbie's throat, ripping out his larynx. Once again, she could see her hairy hand and razor claw, but nobody else could.

The ditsy concubine in the front seat widened her eyes, but made no effort to scream or escape. What she had just witnessed absolutely terrified her, but she was currently unable to decipher what was realism and what was part of her drug-induced trip. Though the blonde trollop couldn't see Dawn's wolf-like attributes, she had watched Dawn remove his voice box with her bare hand and chew on it as if it were a hunk of salt water taffy.

"What size are you?" Dawn asked the conspicuous hussy, looking up to make eye contact while her mouth was smeared with blood.

Minutes later, Dawn deposited the two limp bodies in a dumpster that was conveniently located in the public parking garage, after she was finished helping herself to what she needed. The hired chauffeur and his shameless whore laid there, among the other waste and rubbish, with their entrails hanging out for the spectating world to gander. She had eradicated them both, as savagely as she could. She had, however, shown more mercy to the young vixen, making her demise cleaner and swifter. Both individuals prided themselves on being astute, but they had no idea who or what they were dealing with, when they scorned Dawn. She noticed that one of his glittery, silk, purple stockings had slipped off and gotten left behind on the not-nearly-as squalid ground.

"I hope you had soul," she said to the dead bodies, walking away from the large trash receptacle. "You're going to need it," she added, now wearing the tramp's clothes, which included double-striped tube socks and a long-sleeved baseball jersey that had pink sleeves and neckline, which screened an *iron-on* 8"x10" glossy image of Farrah Fawcett-Majors on the white front. Dawn chose to keep her modified hot pants, which were so short, that the bottom half of her ass cheeks were hanging out and the denim was riding up her butt crack. It was her rare thread of fortune that the floozy's feet matched her size as well.

Purloining what cash they had in his fat wallet and her leather tooled purse, she got back in his taxi and drove to the nearest bus station. This money, along with the bread she had collected from pick-pocketing the recently deceased, allotted her enough to finance a trip to Lexington, Kentucky, and still have some leftover. After making her purchase at the ticket counter, she kneeled down to re-lace and better tie her newly acquired black and white *Converse One Star* sneakers.

Now that she had a pair of dependable tennis shoes, she felt more at ease with the idea of having to dart and dash through the woods. Dawn was rapidly learning to take care of and handle herself, and did so progressively well, but…she wasn't immortal or invincible. She was also not so naive to think for a second that there weren't threats out there, who were considerably more dangerous than she.

Dawn drove the yellow cab a mile down the road and parked it in front of a *Dutch Pantry* restaurant. As she shut the car door behind her, she observed a young man smoking outside of his car, who was leering at her as if he wanted her for dessert. Dawn had become quite the little scamp, and had neither time nor patience for her myriad of male admirers. Linda's ghost once again manifested and produced a sonorous wail, as Dawn cracked a sinister smile. It's not that Dawn enjoyed seeing her mother as a spiritual banshee, but she had been so desensitized and disheartened by life, that Linda couldn't spook or reach her.

Moments later, Dawn walked her sweet ass back to *Greyhound* and waited at the indoor bus stop, holding the ticket she had just bought. She was wearing the guy's gray, hooded sweat jacket, and had left the body next to his car with his throat slit and his dick hard. Dawn had helped herself to inheriting the guy's suede rucksack, which he had sitting on the passenger's seat. Uncertain of the wait she was facing, she takes a load off and sits between two people on the bench. The place is overcrowded, as if she had decided to travel at the worst possible time. She notices that the Korean woman, sitting on her right, is reading the newspaper. There is also a different periodical laying on the woman's lap. Dawn sees that her Falls Church massacre had made national news, as she found herself the primary subject of a headline in both the *New York Post* and the *Pittsburgh Post-Gazette.* The word was out, and she was a star.

Dawn knew that she would be hunted for her display of brutal fatality back at the hospital. She estimated that it would only be a matter of time before she was trapped, so the only thing she could do in the meantime was make it as hard for them as she could. As she sat and waited, between the unpleasant sweat and body odor, she found herself wishing she had taken a train instead. Bored and uncomfortable, she attempted to alleviate her awkwardness by fidgeting her thumbs, as she folded her hands together on her lap. Trying to avoid making eye contact with anyone, hoping to avoid being recognized, she pulled the gray hood as far as it would go over her forehead, and started to stare at her hand. As she held it in front of her, she took turns looking at either side. In her eyes, she still saw hair and claws, but to everyone else…she had a normal human hand. Dawn's mind was gone, and her humanity was clearly out the window. Reuben had been the one treasure to fall into her lap, but

God saw fit to take as quickly as he had given. Dawn would make sure that God paid for putting a hex on her that she could never take off.

Men, women, and children alike, all stare at her as if she was the erotic version of the *Mona Lisa*. She wasn't seen as a barbaric monster, but as a dazzling specimen. Her short shorts certainly didn't help her not be noticed. As she sits on the bus, she looks in the clouded window beside her, and descries hoary streaks in her hair, mainly affecting her front bangs and around the back ends. She rushes to the on-board restroom, and locks the door behind her. She slides her hood back and skittishly runs her clammy hands through her hair, only to wind up with clumps of it in her hands. What perplexes her even more is that, as much as it sheds, it immediately grows back after falling out.

"Hmm," she said, as she picked something off the floor, which she spotted laying between the dirty sink and the even filthier toilet. It looked to be a brochure of sorts, and as she unfolded it, she interpreted it to be appropriate fortuity. It was an educational pamphlet on astrology, particularly on the full moon and how it relates and connects to Mars and the Ram, which were both tied to her Aries birthday. She briefly considered lending her attention to this metaphysical concept, but the flirt was fleeting. She dropped it, leaving it where she had found it, and returned to her economy seat.

Agent Shelling shows up at Reverend Moon's domicile, in what looks to be a normal suburb of Silver Spring. There are several motorcycles parked in front of the abode, along with even more secrets buried underneath it. Mingan answers Shelling's knock, and shows up at the door wearing ceremonial regalia that is made of brown buffalo hide. He is covered in roots, claws, fangs, horns, feathers, and furs. His hair is long and braided, and looks as if it hadn't been washed in quite a while.

"Reverend Moon?"

"Yes?" the Chief answered, while emitting an odor that smelled like a combination of sweetgrass and tobacco.

"My name is Agent Shelling. I'm with the Federal Bureau of Investigations," he properly introduced himself, while showing his badge. "I'm sorry to…" Agent Shelling can barely hear himself talk, as there are loud, totemic instrumentals playing in the background. The observant Reverend turns his head and calls back to his girlfriend to turn down the stereo that is playing the mixed compact cassette. "I'm sorry, Reverend. Is this a bad time? Am I interrupting something?"

"I am sorry. My tribe has come to have a domestic powwow, in honor of my recent engagement to my aponi."

"I see. Well, congratulations, Chief. I don't mean to bother you, but I'm investigating a massacre that your daughter is suspected of committing," he briefed the surprisingly indifferent father on the situation.

"Dawn?" the apathetic Reverend asked, fraudulently posing as being distraught.

"I'm afraid so, Reverend. I'm sorry."

"No. I'm the one who's sorry. Please, come inside," he invited the Agent into his humble home, holding the screen door open for him.

The living room is permeated with the stench of peyote, which a couple of the houseguests are still smoking and tripping on. There is laughter, rejoicing, and feasting. The ceiling is adorned with sagging, Southwestern quilts. There are lava lamps and dream catchers, and windows made from stained glass. A woman, who appeared to be half Mingan's age, casually brushed past Agent Shelling, wearing a denim vest and a tight mini-skirt made of sackcloth. She had an eagle feather in her beaded headband, and her skirt was hiked up high enough to leave nothing to the imagination. She wasn't wearing any panties, as the bottom half of her butt was exposed. The sexually-frustrated federal Agent took notice, while trying to play it off as if he was too professional to appreciate her perfectly shaped Indian ass. Reverend Mingan wore a bone necklace, while Agent Shelling carried a different bone in his trousers.

"I am truly ashamed to hear of what my daughter has done," the perverted Chief immediately apologized, ploying as if he had no card to play in the lousy hand she was dealt. The counterfeit Reverend wasn't oblivious to Agent Shelling's drooling over his trophy girlfriend, Wanema, but decided to ignore that and concentrate on the Bureau's unwelcome interest in his hopeful prodigal. "My daughter has always had a bit of Sedit in her, I'm afraid. I often suffer this upsetting vision that she has become a malfunctioning member of society, addicted to drugs, sleeping on park benches, and soliciting in dark alleys. What can I do to help?"

Agent Shelling didn't even question what the minister meant by the word, *Sedit*, even though he was completely in the dark, regarding its definition. He found it unsettling and suspicious that the Cherokee widower didn't fight the idea of his only daughter being presumed guilty of such heinous assassinations. The Native preacher didn't seem shocked or bothered that his child was the lead suspect of such horrific atrocities. He had expected to be met with resistance, and figured he'd have to resort to threatening her father with a search warrant, but neither was necessary. It significantly crept him out that the good Reverend was so serene about the pending homicide charges.

"Has she attempted to contact you? Does she have any other family or friends she might seek asylum with?" he asked the Cherokee minister, happy to see him cooperating, but sensing a darkened and even demonic effusion about him.

"No," Reverend Moon answered. "Though, if she did, you know I would have to grant her sanctuary, and would have every legal right to do so. That said, however, I am obliged and obligated to do whatever I can to accommodate you and your laws."

"I will find her," Agent Shelling affirmed, trying to both convince the Reverend and himself.

"You won't find her. Dawn is young, but she's cunning. She knows how to evade and elude predators. You won't be able to track her. She has too much of the wolf spirit in her," her father insisted, not knowing half of the truth he just spoke. The raunchy reverend had just gotten back from losing much of the church's funds, while at a Baltimore casino that he covertly frequented.

"Did Dawn have a happy childhood?" Agent Shelling asked, anxious to hear the Chief's response.

"Absolutely," Reverend Moon promptly replied, lying through his yellowed teeth.

"Do you have a recent photo of your daughter?" he asked the relaxed preacher, while looking at the many displayed, framed pictures of the family. "That is, one which you wouldn't mind letting me have?"

"Absolutely," Mingan acknowledged. "In fact, I have one that was taken just weeks before she was admitted into the mental hospital. I'll go fetch it," he said, leaving the FBI investigator alone in his living room.

Agent Shelling had noticed that the pastor reeked of body odor, and could smell the mixture of cheap liquor and cigar smoke on his fetid breath. He was no one to surmise or chastise anyone, as he had dark sins of his own, but he detected that this man had no business making a living as a man of the cloth. As he waits for the evangelical Chief to return with the photo, he is startled to find another Indian sitting in the lotus position with his eyes closed, as if lost in deep meditation. The man is dressed entirely in faded blue denim, accompanied with a beaded belt, and sterling silver rings on his fingers. As the FBI investigator stares in bewilderment at the ensconced Indian, astonished that he can be at such peace amongst such disturbance, the Indian opened his left eye and returned his focused gaze.

"To find her," he said, "you must first find yourself; and even if you attain that enlightenment, you can't catch a coyote unless she wants to be caught," the mohawk-styled aborigine told the Fed, as he cocks a half smile and laughs, while flicking him off with both hands that had been resting on his knees.

As Agent Shelling begins to feel the effects of the secondhand peyote smoke, his head starts to spin fast, as he turns his attention to the 5"x7" graduation photo that Reverend Moon just handed him. As the dizzy Agent scrutinizes at the school picture, he hallucinates, seeing Dawn become animated in the high school photograph. She rises off the picture, as if a hologram sitting up in its tomb. Dawn's cap and gown fall off her slender body, as she speaks to him.

"You're wasting your time, buckaroo. I'm too fast for you," his optical illusion of Dawn says with fierce intimidation, as he rubs his eyes. Her hair and body are dripping wet with sweat and tears. Her mouth salivates, while she breathes heavily. Her blue eyes roll into the back of her head and the whites turn blood red. Her mouth hangs open to show Agent Shelling her teeth, which are long and sharp. Though her facade was intended to be scary, he could tell that she was scared. What he failed to see, however, was that she wasn't scared of him, but of herself.

"Take me to her room!" Agent Shelling insists, pocketing the talking photograph and barely able to maintain his balance. He knows he has been outwitted, but refuses to leave that domicile without first seeing Dawn's bedroom. He squints his eyes, trying his best to see, despite his temporarily blurred vision. "Take me to her room!" he repeated in a hostile tone, grabbing her father by the collar. "Take me to her room, and I'll leave," he promised. "I swear to God."

Though the drugged Fed could barely walk, Reverend Moon helped him to Dawn's room. Once Agent Shelling moved away from the peyote smoke, he began to regain his composure and stand on his own. He anxiously shifted and snooped through her things, hoping to find something that might help him track her, or at least explain why she became such an animal.

He spotted a delicate jewelry box on top of her dresser, which had a majestic painting of a wolf on the lid. He opened it, and found a matchbook cover from the Waldorf nightclub, *The Moonlight Inn*. As he held it firmly in his closed hand, he could see flashes of her in his mind, of her lounging and flirting inside the club, trying to persuade the men to buy her drinks. She wasn't there for the bands, but for the booze.

As he invaded her privacy by rummaging through her belongings, he stumbled upon a belt that looked unlike any he had seen before. As he held it up to his face, to get a closer and better look at it, he saw that the belt was made of wolf fur and what appeared to be either animal or human skin. He suddenly felt sick, but pleased to see that the belt wasn't made of human vagina, confusing the American Indians for the Islamic tradition of female genital mutilation.

"Do you have any more questions for us?" Rev. Mingan faked being polite, perturbed that the nosy Agent was so interested in his toothsome daughter.

"No," the FBI Agent punctually answered, while covering his mouth as if to keep himself from puking. "I believe I'm done here."

With her brown tote backpack reposed between her feet, Dawn looks out the partially frosted window, as the weather continued to draw nearer to Winter's ruthless disposition. As she left Pennsylvania, her scenery slightly changed. She soon no longer saw coal mines and steel mills, but continued to see country-styled homes sporadically spread alongside the road, clotheslines arranged in the yard, and gas stations with rusted tin signs. There were plenty of mom-n-pop stores advertising homemade pies, and haystack cluttered, open farmland. She even sees a hitchhiker, holding a cardboard sign that says he *will do anything for a ride*. She sighed in fertilized misery and slowly shook her head, in remembrance of her lousy experience as a reluctant nomad.

NOVEMBER 2, 1977
WANING GIBBOUS

The free press had allocated wall-to-wall news coverage to Dawn and her indiscriminate bloodbath. She had swiftly become an urban legend, taking no time at all to climb up the bloody ladder of infamy. The FBI was also proving to be an integral part in turning Dawn's sanguinary crusade into a media frenzy. The chase was on full force, and she was hastily making a name for herself as a serial killer. As families watched on their tubular televisions and intently listened to their portable *Philips* radios, the impuissant nation was advised to stay indoors and be on constant lookout for the sensual, but sinister, Indian-flavored basket case.

The police switchboard is swamped with calls, testifying to exaggerated near-death sightings and accurately describing Dawn's titillating package. Line-ups become a daily routine, never leading anywhere, as they bring in any female off the street who has olive or tan skin. The police and the Feds get lost in being overwhelmed and disorganized, as they struggle to coordinate between each other, with faxes, blood samples, and the like.

The FBI coaxes a national radio show to offer Dawn an enticing deal on the air, that is illegitimate, but fetching all the same. This effort is to bribe her with perks and pledges of exoneration, if she simply phones in, to share her side of the story (hoping to keep her on the line for a minimum of 15 minutes, to trace her location and get it recorded). The telephone rings, and it becomes a race on who can answer it first.

"Get ready to roll tape!" one of the lead investigators shouts, in optimistic presumption that it is who they want it to be.

"Offer the anger management class!" another clamors out, authorizing an alternate scheme to get Dawn to turn herself in.

It's a telemarketer, who not only interferes with the federal operation, but both disappoints and infuriates the sanctioned authorities. Dawn never calls, or falls for the devious trick, as she is sharper than the eagle and smarter than any coyote.

Agent Shelling slouches in his swivel chair, languid and despondent. He thought about his son, and how he had never come home from Vietnam. The war was over, but his only child was still missing. His nephew had therefore grown to fill that void, and become the son that he feared he'd never see again. He wanted Dawn's head so bad, that he could figuratively taste the flavor of her coveted blood in his hydrophobic mouth. He dismayed, however, that his relentless pursuit of her would turn out to be nothing more than a pipe dream, which he could never accomplish or conquer. About three hours later, following the failed radio scam, one of Agent Shelling's many superiors gave a press announcement. They had expeditiously learned that Dawn couldn't be schemed or manipulated, so there was no longer any rational logic in keeping the black cat in the proverbial bag.

"Although this strange girl doesn't appear to fit the profile of typical, criminal-pattern behavior, we have come to an unanimous conclusion. Since receiving flooded feedback on our tip line, we have confirmed that Dawn Moon *is* the serial killer we have been looking for," the obnoxious Lieutenant addressed, endorsing the suspicions. "We have the entire task force working on this case. We will find her. It's only a question of when," the homicide detective reassured the general public and vengeful Uncle.

The truth was that neither the police department, nor the Bureau, could honestly substantiate their allegations against their prime suspect. They had some solid evidence, but none of it was strong enough to prosecute. This was fine with Agent Shelling, as he would much rather envision her dead than incarcerated, and wasn't overly concerned with the status of her guilt. He just wanted someone to pay for the atrocity done to his disturbed nephew, and he was determined to make sure that someone suffered the cost and consequence. As the press conference ended, with the FBI making empty threats of guaranteeing the gas chamber, the district attorney watched as Agent Shelling carried on into the falling dusk.

Dawn spent the night walking the streets, and getting into cars of those who were either notorious or rancorous. She consented to the rides and performed for a price, lowering her standards and discarding her morals, because she was desperate for the income. Though she couldn't explain why it was or how she knew, Dawn was confident that she was somehow immune to contracting sexually-transmitted diseases...and she was right. Her cells were changing faster than she could think, and though she would never be immortal or indestructible, she was becoming stronger in ways, while weaker in others. Her blood had developed certain biological resilience, including a natural version of penicillin. She could have easily just butchered these men and taken their money, but she felt sympathetic towards them, as most of her johns were souls who were forlorn and broken. Once she had earned enough, she used the cash to shell out for an airline ticket from the newly opened *Blue Grass Airport*. It didn't take her long to pick a destination, as an inner voice led her to choosing Albuquerque, New Mexico.

Before Dawn entered the airport, she was having some trouble, sliding and slipping on the ice. The Bluegrass State had frozen over, which made her feel even better about relocating further West. As she casually walks toward the terminal doors, she sees a shuttle carelessly hit and run over a Siberian Husky, and not because of problems with hydroplaning or standing water. Dawn stops and stands there, while she watches the driver get out of the short bus, and senselessly kick the marred canine body, before he disrespectfully and callously steps over it. Dawn is repulsed, as she witnesses him leave the road kill there, like the innumerable hunters who kill for the brutal sport. She follows him into the terminal, keeping a safe distance behind, as not to be suspected. She tracks this killer to a restroom. She waits for him to go inside, and then enters herself. As soon as she does, a couple of middle-aged guys promptly leave. Dawn steps up to the airport transporter, where he is holding himself up at one of the urinals. He's so self-absorbed, that her very presence escapes him. He is wearing a filthy, white, thermal-underwear top that looks as if it had never been washed; and an open flannel shirt over it. He had an unzipped fur coat atop everything, which was posh and authentic. He had camouflage suspenders that held up faded, baggy denim pants, which were fashionably ornamented with holes and stains. He had on black combat boots, that clearly came from a surplus store, and a backwards ball cap that was in the design of the Confederate rebel flag.

Her mother's wraith appeared again, looking exactly like she did when she died. Linda's hair was long, and parted down the middle. It was short on the very top, but as her layered hair fell around her, it was feathered and wavy on the sides. She wailed like a banshee, as her way of desperately pleading with Dawn to stop her death wish. Once again, Dawn ignored her warning.

"So, did you have fun?" she asked him, already knowing the answer. "I just bet you have animal skins and heads on your walls, don't you? You think we're prizes, or trophies, for you to poach and possess? We're called *wildlife* for a reason, asshole! You like kicking dogs? You're the dog…you son of a bitch."

Not expecting to hear a girl's voice in the Men's room, the grossly overweight public servant turned around to meet his stalker. Before he could discern who was speaking to him, she had already seized the presumed taxidermist by the throat and fiercely bashed the back of his skull against the tiled wall. She dropped the bloodied man, letting his fractured head hit the side of the urinal tank on the way down. Suddenly feeling sick to her stomach, Dawn leaned forward and vomited on his face. Just then, a Muslim man walks in and sees this scene of reprehensible horror before him. Before he could utter a word or cry for help, Dawn lunges at him, clasping him by his corporate suit and throwing him against the wall. She goes over and stands beside him, using her foot to press masterfully against his smug face.

"You know, the only thing I agree with your religion on, is your practice of stoning adulterers. I get that. I really do. That said, I have to kill you for your insolence, which I refuse to tolerate. You're familiar with that feeling, right? Intolerance?" she asks, rhetorically and sarcastically.

She presses down on the Muslim's head, effortlessly snapping his neck with her delicate foot, not even noticing her mother's crying-ghost anymore. Linda was trying to save her obstinate daughter from plummeting further into the depths of lunacy, but her efforts were unavailing. Linda's hindsight was lucid as crystal, and she hankered to be there for her child, the way that she regretted lacking during life. Haplessly, Dawn was too far gone, and destined for the path of self-destruction.

Dawn figured that leaving from a distant airport would be preferable, as she calculated that the odds of her being watched would be much lower. She was partially correct, but not entirely out of the fire. Though nobody was there looking for her, she was most undoubtedly the sight to behold, but only out of unadulterated concupiscence. As Dawn walked to her terminal, she turned heads from both genders, as they gawked ravenously at her succulent and nubile figure. Dawn's headshot was being flashed and publicized over the small screen, as the state and federal law enforcement did whatever they could to sully her name with libelous stories, which only carried thin threads of veracity. Notwithstanding, most only looked at her as an object of desire, not as public enemy number one.

While Dawn waited patiently at her Gate, assorted men find the two bloodied corpses in the restroom, but nobody makes a move to react to or report the discovery. Even those who want to do something, cowardly look at the ground or go about their own business. They see that one of the mutilated is a Muslim, and refrain from acting, out of fear of being questioned themselves or mislabeled a racist.

A little boy is playing with his *Mego* 13" Paul Stanley doll and *Mego* 12" Batman doll. He is standing up in his seat and turned around, so he can perform a puppet show of sorts, using the top of the back of his seat as center stage. The kid is using his two toys to shoot at each other, even though neither plastic icon is equipped with a little gun. He then turns his attention to Dawn and begins play-shooting her, while she looks understandably irked in the seat behind him.

Once Dawn is able to block out the little brat, and drift off to dreamland, she sleeps like the dead. She practically sleeps through the whole *Pan Am* flight, perfectly content and comfortable in Coach. Dawn isn't the typical young woman who is impressed by glittery and shiny materialism. Aside from being a homicidal maniac, she is actually quite the catch, as she is anything but shallow or fickle. At one point, the contemptible boy pelts his *KISS* doll at Dawn, striking her directly in the forehead, which somehow falls short of disrupting or waking her.

As Dawn stepped out of the *Albuquerque International Sunport*, she admired the large Southwestern statue out front. The impressive sculpture was of a winged man who was in mid-dance, as if participating in some tribal celebration. As she walks further away from the airport, she spots a biker mounting his ride. It was a 1947 Indian Chief *Roadmaster*, painted in powdered blue and ivory white. She was in wonderment of its beauty, and longed to know the working condition of the classic bike. As the imitation outlaw was getting on the leather saddle, he nearly fell clean off, seeing her suddenly standing in front of his prized hog.

"Holy shit!" he shouted, "where the fuck did you come from?!" he inquired, unnerved that he never heard or saw her coming.

"I dig your bike," she said, in a demeanor which implied that she wasn't leaving without it.

"Well, I like your tits," the biker boldly answered back, attempting to disguise his awkward fear with crude humor. "Turn around, baby, so I can see if your ass is as nice," he added, faking a smile to throw her off his intimidated scent.

She was thoroughly impressed by his chrome chariot, but not by him. He wasn't used to women not being nervous, shy, or easy. Chicks often either feared him or took off their tops for him; either, he was accustomed to owning the attention and control. Dawn wasn't going to move out of the way, and he picked up on that. He kicked up the metal stand and began to gradually walk the cherished bike backward, putting distance between them. He kept a close eye on her, while he backed the cycle several yards from where she stood. As he started the engine, he found Dawn standing right beside him. This time he did fall off, frightened of her, not having seen her move an inch from where she had been.

"Please, he said," now showing his true colors, as he trembled and begged, "Don't take my bike. It's all I have left."

"I'm sorry," she apologized, "but I'm afraid I need it more than you."

The tattooed poser felt his pounding heart, as it resounded and rose up his throat, while he watched her blue eyes turn pitch black, just long enough to literally scare the shit out of him. He was so consumed with ultimate terror, that his panicked thoughts never devoted a millisecond to feeling embarrassed about messing his trousers. He continued to look her in the eyes, which had already returned to the pretty blue, but retained a menacing threat that pierced his inner child like a burning blade.

"If you tell anyone about this," she gave fair warning, "I will be back, and will make you sorry. Are we clear?"

"Yes," he promptly replied, slowly nodding his head, while still lying on the ground. He believed her threat, and she could see that. He had no intention of ever telling a soul, which was what ultimately saved his life.

Dawn hastily found herself riding her hijacked motorcycle down the highway, with the wind in her hair and freedom in her horizon. She rode like Evel Knievel, throwing caution to the wind and letting go…at least momentarily…of her doubts, worries, and fears. She had no premeditated destination, but just knew that she wanted to keep heading West.

Agent Shelling shows up at the *Dutch Pantry* restaurant parking lot, in Pittsburgh, following through on a witness sighting that matched Dawn's description. The city police are there, and he sees a chalk drawing of where her victim was discovered. The cops are dumbfounded at the discovered corpse, and couldn't begin to explain what had ripped out the man's throat.

"I can't tell what direction the stab wound is in," the forensics specialist admitted.

"Stab wound?! Where do you see evidence of a stab wound? This wasn't from any large knife or sharp tool, but from something of a different nature altogether," the frustrated Deputy Commissioner openly vented, pulling his hair out from each side of his aching head. "And why the fuck is the victim aroused?! Who gets a hard-on from being butchered?!" He then turned around to see Agent Shelling standing right behind him. "What the hell is the FBI doing here?! Goddammit! As if I don't have enough shit to fucking worry about!!" he added, in furious aggravation and annoyance, as he walked away from the Fed. Agent Shelling followed him.

"The suspect, in question, is a female serial killer who initiated her murder spree at a psychiatric ward in Northern Virginia. The Bureau was called in to help, because the mental patients were from different states and jurisdictions," Agent Shelling began to justify his presence.

"Yeah, I don't buy that. You must have a personal stake in this case, right? I'm guessing you have a dog in this fight. Am I right?" Chief Deputy Plant asked, turning out to be more intuitive than he could have possibly imagined.

"Just doing my job," Agent Shelling claimed. "It's my duty to investigate every possible lead, and I fully intend to do that. This was what I signed up for."

"Well, I hope you've had your breakfast already, because this is the worst atrocity I've ever seen. The victim's throat was gutted. His neck and face are completely mangled, and nearly decapitated. I'd be fascinated to get this bitch into interrogation, mainly because we can't figure out the weapon she used to do this, or why there are semen stains on the victim's pants," the Deputy Commissioner added. "We can't let the locals get wind of this. It would cause a statewide panic of chaotic proportions."

Had it not been for the SNAFU urgency of the grisly extermination, at the Virginian psychiatric facility,

Agent Shelling would be on a non-related assignment, forced to focus on a case that wasn't such a conflict of interest. His sister's son was a good lad, didn't deserve what he had been dealt, and should have never been in that mental hospital. This enraged Agent Shelling even more, that his wronged nephew wound up being a casualty of the contained genocide. Rumors were spreading like wildfire that William's death had been part of a Satanic sacrifice, and that the whole bloodletting that day had been ritualistically motivated. Though it appeared that Agent Shelling was playing pocket pool, he was in fact playing with an arrow head that belonged to her evangelical father, which he had pickpocketed from their house while prodding and goading Dawn's family in Silver Spring.

"He wasn't even supposed to be there," he mumbled under his breath, referring to his pilfered nephew again, convinced that William had been inequitably tagged and confined.

"I'm sorry, sir. What was that?" one of the detectives asked the troubled Agent.

Agent Shelling then found a clump of hair on the asphalt, next to the victim's car, that looked and felt identical to the wolf hair samples found at the psychiatric hospital.

"Oh, umm, nothing," he lied to the detective. "I was just saying to myself that I wish I could have a cold beer."

"Yeah, I hear that," the detective chuckled and snorted. "Don't we all."

Agent Shelling knew that if word got out that his nephew was among the murdered lunatics, that it would not only look bad on him, but would lead to questions he'd rather not face. He couldn't let that happen, as he was determined to devote the rest of his life to hunting down William's killer. Each time he showed up to dissect another body or survey another fatality, he kept seeing William's face on each of Dawn's victims. Like the radical Islamic theology, he was the epitome of hatred and subversion, whether it was warranted or not.

"I will find your slayer, William," he said out loud, though talking to nobody in particular other than himself. "As God as my witness, I will track that fucking bitch down!" he said arrogantly, presuming that Dawn was the culprit and not the suspect.

Dawn darted down *Highway 85*, weaving in and out of the lanes at her leisure. Riding the *Roadmaster* gave her a thrill she couldn't verbally express, which permitted her to temporarily pretend that her life of loss and disappointment wasn't too painful to bear or cope with. Being on the run gave her excitement, while sitting on the motorcycle let her make believe that her future wasn't written and that she had control over her destiny. It was just after midnight now, and she had passed several retail markets, where she was tempted to stop and switch license plates, but wisely declined. If she made any move to alter the bike's identity, it wouldn't matter if the owner squealed on her or not. No, she needed to trust that her fierce warning had been enough to ensure her incognito status. Changing the tags, at this point, would only leave a trail of clues for the police to follow.

She speeds down the highway, like a bat out of Hell, whizzing between the automotive congestion. A dreadful and disgraceful couple, in their late 20s, are stuck in the slow-moving traffic. The male element of the unhinged twosome, who was almost equally as toxic as his female counterpart, saw Dawn coming up in their rearview mirror. He waited until Dawn got close to his truck and then opened the door, deliberately causing Dawn to fly off the saddle and be thrown yards in front of their pickup. The guy was bald on the top of his head, and could barely spell the word, *dog*, yet somehow managed to retain the affections of his easy wife, who was warm on the outside but gelid around the heart. He was as ugly on the surface as she was on the inside, thereby making them the perfect match. They had a mini gun rack, bolted to the back of the truck, which holstered two shotgun rifles. The conniving couple cackled in mockery and amusement, but their blissful victory would be short-lived. Dawn, barely dinged up, rose to her feet and stared at the joyful pair, while clinching her fists in anticipated retribution. Everyone within view, felt as if they were trapped in a state of collective surrealism, as they watched Dawn approach the rusted, dust-ridden truck.

"Mark! What the fuck?! How is that bitch still alive?" Heather asked, disappointed that her husband's unprovoked road rage was unsuccessful. "You can't fucking do anything right, can you? I can't believe I left my third husband for you!" she yells, as she plays with the cross of gold around her neck, which represented her faux faith, and symbolized the insincerity of her commitment to the Lord and every poor husband she'd ever use.

"Shut the fuck up, you lowlife skank," Mark replied. "You were cheating with me since before you and he ever met, much less got married. You're a fraud and a cunt, who uses and damages people, who do nothing but love you. You have never given a shit about anyone but yourself," he gruffly retorted, putting his scam-artist spouse in her place.

"Then why are you with me, then?!" the blonde Heather yelled back, insulted that he accused her of being a monster, which she knew she was and was proud to be. "I have three kids, you son of a bitch! You don't think I love them?! They call you *Daddy*!"

"Yeah, they called Nick 'Daddy' too once, Heather. How many *Daddies* are your kids gonna have? What the hell do you think you're teaching them?" Mark answered. "You're only 27, and you've been married four times. You pretended to be with Nick for five years, and all you ever did was secretly betray him with me, and embezzle money from him and his daughter. You're an identity thief, for Christ' sake. You're trash, Heather. You're a snake," he admitted, having no idea that she had been married more than just four times, and was a polygamist on top of everything else.

"Why the fuck are you with me then?!" Heather repeated her question, glaring angrily at the man who was basically her pimp.

"You're a nice package, Heather…you're just an empty one. I'm with you because you're good in the sack, and I don't care about people any more than you do, which is why I agreed to sleep with you while I was still married to my wife. Just don't fucking play your games with me. I'm not one of your dimwitted suckers."

"Fuck you, asshole! I want a divorce!" she exclaimed, as usual not willing to discuss her selfish and sadistic agenda, when called on and confronted about it.

"Wow, what a shocker. I suppose it's my turn, huh?" he said, pointing out how pathetically easy it was for her to dump her meaningless marriages. "Do you even know who the true father is of your children? Are they really the offspring of your first husband? Or, are they secretly the result of the multitude of men you cheated on Jason with?" he asked her, once again being met with unfeeling silence. "Holy shit," Mark said, learning something new about the demon he thought he knew so well. "You don't know who the father is, do you? You don't know if there is more than one, and what's worse…you couldn't care less. You used Jason the same way you used Nick, and you are all too proud of yourself for what you did to damage both families. Jason didn't abuse you any more than Nick did. They both loved you with all their hearts, and you took joy from making them pay for that mistake. I thought I was cold, Heather…but you have redefined the word, *heartless.*"

Just then, Dawn had torn off the hood to their hayseed truck, using nothing but her own two hands. Mark's and Heather's eyes widened in sheer disbelief, as their lovers' quarrel was cut short by the sight of Dawn holding the heavy hunk of metal. They watched as Dawn threw the hood several feet off the Southern Route, not unlike how Heather had once thrown away Nick and his seven-year-old child. The difference was, Dawn wasn't callous or ruthless, but just fed up.

The aspiring prostitute opened her door, like Nick had always opened doors for her, but tried to make a run for it instead of being polite. She was prepossessing in the face, but a bit on the heavy side, so she could only run so fast. Dawn watched her scram towards the cars behind them and scream, as she begged for someone to stop and help her. Luckily, no one wanted to lend a hand, and in fact locked their doors as they saw Heather coming with her feigned tears. You could tell that she wasn't wearing any underwear, as her pants rode up the crack of her flat ass. Heather banged on windows, hoping that she would eventually encounter a police vehicle who would be more willing to aid her. Mark, on the other hand, being the true coward he was, couldn't even muster up the courage to go for one of his rifles, which were foolishly displayed on the outside of the back of the cab, making them ineffective and inaccessible. Dawn stepped up to the driver's side and knocked on Mark's window. The flow of traffic had begun to move again, but Mark had pissed his pants and was too frozen in fear to apply the gas pedal.

"Get out of the truck," Dawn demanded, as the other commuters courteously refrained from browbeating or honking, but rather made their way around the pickup, as if in unspoken agreement that this was a battle they'd wish to stay out of. Dawn saw that the other travelers were making a real effort to not interfere with or infuriate her, so she picked up her bike and moved it out of their way, to show her appreciation. Dawn knocked on Mark's window again, but saw that he wasn't going to budge. She could smell his fear, which was more potent than his body odor or the stink leftover from Heather's communal vagina. Dawn cupped her hand to her forehead, while leaning up against the side window. She saw open boxes of clothes, which included a brown suede fringe jacket. She noticed that none of the clothes looked to be the same size and that the assorted variety was too widespread to cater solely to their tastes. "Where are all the clothes from?" she asked the flea-infested Mark, through his window, which was still rolled up.

"My wife takes clothes from schools and churches," he said, now able to speak, but still too petrified to drive off. "She likes to take her kids to different pageants and parties, so she can rob the people there, while they're distracted."

"I bet you want one of your guns, don't you?" she asked the sweaty, wrestling fan. "What kind of imbecile keeps his weapons on the outside of his truck? Seriously?"

"I don't know?" the honkytonk patron answered back.

"Did you know that guns were once called *peacemakers*?" Dawn asked her natural adversary. "Hunting does not contribute to peace, you arrogant, selfish mother fucker."

"Yes, mam," he acknowledged her. "You're right. I'm so sorry."

"I'll tell you what," she said. "What size is that fringe jacket?"

Dawn had resumed her journey, enjoying her new motorcycle, which miraculously appeared to be as unharmed as she was. She left Mark to his own pathetic existence, and had considered chasing Heather, but took solace in knowing that her time would come and that Karma would catch up to her eventually. She just wished that she could be there to see Heather get what was coming to her, but was wise enough to know that God doesn't allow us that pleasure. Mark waited awhile for Heather, but figured that she probably used her seductive charms to get a ride from some other gullible or vulnerable fool. Mark took off, deciding that he would be better off without the conceited skank, and would keep an eye out for someone who closer resembled the naked silhouette on his mud flaps.

DECEMBER 25, 1977
COLD MOON

It's Christmas Day, and like many in America, Dawn was dejected and disconsolate, as none of the holiday decorations or festivities made up for the inner torment she felt without her pale-skinned piece of gingerbread. She kept telling herself that he wasn't gone, but that they were only temporarily separated. She knew that as long as she loved and remembered him, he would never truly be dead. Regardless of what the future had in store, or whom she ended up with later on, Reuben would always be the definition of her heart. Nothing would ever change that, and nobody would ever come between them. Dawn wasn't like many women, when it came to relationships. When she loved, she loved faithfully and forever.

Dawn had been in El Paso for a month and a half, and was getting hungry and lonely. She would take money here and there, from both johns and victims, but only spent it when she absolutely needed it and if there was no other recourse. She tried to save even more of her limited funds by sleeping in dark alleyways with the derelicts and the rats. She tried her best not to feed, as she understood that her only chance of maintaining her liberty was to stop killing. Then again, she had to consider her basic survival. Dawn had reluctantly broken down and sold the motorcycle, though it killed her to do so. Trying to avoid attracting more attention, she even fought to get employment as a dogman, but the foreman laughed at her, in front of the crew, when she insisted that she would have no problem lifting and moving heavy pipes. She occasionally tried to eat normal food, hoping that things had changed, but her taste for it never returned.

Dawn considers legally changing her name, but decides that it would only leave a paper trail, which would only complicate things and place her deeper at risk. She contemplates looking for a job, but realizes that making a legitimate income would only help the FBI track her whereabouts. She resorts to sticking with the oldest profession, where giving a social security number isn't required and a background check isn't mandatory. Dawn didn't get pleasure from hooking, and it certainly didn't make her jubilant, but she was fresh out of choices. She was faced with either selling her body or selling her soul, and the thought of the latter paralyzed her. The rotation of dusk and daybreak had become an endless hourglass, where Dawn stayed on guard and fought to never surrender. Though part of her was already dead, if she were to be honest, she knew she couldn't deny her thanatophobia. Her own mortality terrified her, as she believed in both the afterlife and in

God, neither of which were nearly as comforting as she would have liked.

She wasn't as piqued with Texas as she would have preferred, but she was growing fond of the Lone Star State, which so far seemed to offer an environment that was peaceful and quiet. Little did she know that she had judged it prematurely, as the chickens were just about to be counted. She woke up one morning, to hear boisterous commotion coming from across the street from where she had shacked up the night before. She had stayed in a room at the *Coral Motel*, for a couple of nights, which had been a nice change of pace from laying with the vagrants, even though the trick who was flipping the bill was vulgar and disparaging. It was his fetish to make her feel debased and degraded, along with indulging in the S&M scene with younger and prettier girls like Dawn. She didn't fancy being a streetwalker, nor was she proud of herself for keeping johns like him alive; but it was keeping her going and he was loaded. He had just gagged her with his fat, sweaty cock, and had finished in her mouth. One of the stranger things he was into, was having his whores kiss him while they hold his sperm in their mouth, and then having them open wide, so he could spit it back in their mouths for them to swallow. As Dawn remains on her knees, waiting for him to return his load to her waiting mouth, he noticed that several of her teeth were jagged, and even pointed.

"Christ Almighty!" he blurted out, as intentionally insensitive as possible. "No man's going to marry you with that fucking grill. I'm shocked that you didn't chew off my dick?!"

"I have no interest in marriage," she said, knowing she'd never love anyone the way she does Reuben, nor would she ever have reason to promise her life to anyone but Reuben.

"Well, that's probably a good thing, with you having shark teeth and a public pussy. No man wants a fucking slut that's been used like a cum dumpster. Besides, they say that relationships that start off in adultery, always end in disaster."

"Well, if that's what they say, then they aren't very bright. Either that, or they haven't been paying attention."

"Why do you say that?" he asked her, confused on what she meant.

"Are you kidding me? I've personally watched and known countless women, who proudly throw their relationships and marriages away for the men they shamelessly cheat with, only to still be with those despicable men years later, down the road, happy and content. So, whatever counselor or minister that told you that statistic is full of shit."

While her heavy suitor slept like the dead, she heard a concerning uproar that came from outside but sounded as if it was right beside her. She got up out of bed, got dressed, and began to walk across the street to see what the pandemonium was all about. After stepping outdoors, she happened upon a stick, that looked a bit like nature's pitchfork. She curiously bent over to pick up the uncanny wood, and as she did, she felt an electric charge rush through her body. The shot of electricity had implanted an idea in her head. Straightening her posture, she resumed her walking, but now using the stick as a compass. Like a blind person with a white cane, she relied on the forked stick to guide her. Stupefied by it all, she followed its lead.

The motel was embellished with a fuchsia neon sign in front of it and a clayish-vermillion roof above. The inn was literally off US-62, and very convenient to shopping and dining amenities. Dawn jogged over the first three-lane road, until she reached the dividing island. She waited for a break in traffic, as she looked at the scattered plant life, which included a midget palm tree or two. When it was safe, she crossed the next three-lane roadway, which went the opposite direction. Dawn soon found herself in an outlet mall, which catered to different needs and tastes. There was a quaint little Mexican cafe, a *Waxie Maxies* record store, a *Wicks N' Sticks*, a thrift clothing store, and a shelter for battered women. There was a single billboard posted over this lot, proudly advertising for *Smith & Wesson*. She saw a bus stop, a bench, and a *Kmart*.

Among all of this was what appeared to be a gutted gym, which the thunderous sound was clearly coming from. Dawn stepped inside of what had, at one time, been a training center for amateur fighters. Everything had been taken out, leaving the place open for criminal activities. It had since been converted to a despicable den of animal abuse. There was a crowd there, mainly consisting of hunters and poachers. They were cheering on one of the countless dogfights they regularly hosted there. This particular dogfight was between a leather-brownish pit bull and a white timber wolf. The pit bull had its' mouth covered with blood. It snarled at the wolf with a menacing glare that would intimidate a black bear. This pit bull, much like the other dogs, had been bred to bite and hold around the head. Dawn saw dead dogs that were laying on the floor, in different areas of the arena, with their faces looking as if they had been put through a meat grinder. This was considered to be compliment held in high regard, as the more gamey the loser, the better the defeat. Dawn dropped her forked stick, sickened by this repugnant sport.

These men and women who orchestrated these dogfights, prided themselves as sportsmen, but were abominable human beings. The dogs would be starved, beaten, kicked, whipped with chains, and often forced to feed on the losing dogs. Not only were these dogs unspeakably maltreated to make them vicious and savage, but the monsters who put these fights on, made it known that they received joyful bliss from causing and watching these dogs murder each other. The whole bloody scene was unsettling and unforgivable. When Dawn courageously stepped inside this mock-coliseum, her eyes immediately began to water. The ruthless gamblers were screaming and cheering, while waving their blood-money high in the air, to celebrate the indecent bets they had committed to, based on who they believed could best match their blood thirst. Dawn's eyes were immediately drawn to the white wolf, as he and the pit bull circled around each other, as if to try and psyche each other out before their attack.

The audience members were all bathed in dried mud, as were their vests and trucks. The only ones in the room who weren't flea-ridden were the dogs and the wolf. Dawn was initially petrified in denial, finding all this to be too sensationally horrible to be real. As she watched the two snarl and stare at each other, while they continued to build themselves up for the kill, it took every effort for Dawn not to jump in and assist the wolf. She really wanted to lend a hand, but something held her back, as if she somehow knew that he was capable of handling his own. After several moments of procrastination, Dawn decides to intervene, but before she gets her chance, the white wolf ends up winning the fight without much damage to himself. Dawn is completely mystified by the wolf's vivid and hypnotic yellow eyes, as he briefly makes eye contact with her.

Dawn watches a cluster of thugs tackle the wolf and restrain him with a muzzle and shackles. The goons roughly load him in the back of a tinted van, and haul him away down the road. Dawn follows close behind, but keeping safe distance as not to be detected, as they lead her to a seemingly normal ranch. She waits until nightfall, and then breaks into the stable where the wolf is being chained. Dawn snaps the chain with her bare hands, and frees the wolf from bondage. The wolf runs out of the barn, and Dawn walks over to the dark farmhouse. She barricades the doors and sets the place on fire, with a full gas can and a cigarette lighter that she found in a tool shed nearby. She grins in satisfaction, as she can hear the detestable family of pseudo-Christians scream for help that never comes, as they burn alive inside.

"For you are dust, and to dust you shall return," she said, quoting Genesis 3:19.

Dawn turns around to see the white wolf snarling and drooling at her, staring at her as if he wanted to rip her to shreds and ultimately devour her. While anyone else would have been petrified with fear or run for their very life, Dawn looked through this defensive charade and saw behind the wolf's mask. She could sense his wretched woe, and could see that he was gentle, and even altruistic, beneath the guise of antipathy and animosity.

"You're just as afraid as I am, aren't you, boy?" she asked, careful to use a soothing and non-threatening voice. She wanted him to know that she respected him, and meant him no harm.

The wolf's irate eyes didn't change, making it clear that he didn't trust her. She didn't take it personally, as she could see that it was humans in general that he had been programmed to be weary of. Dawn remembered that she had pocketed some red rose pedals from her travels thus far, which she had boldly picked from private property here and there. She slowly reached in her jacket pocket and pulled out the pedals, which she then showed to the wolf.

"See," she said. "They're just flowers. It's okay, gorgeous. They're just flowers."

Though Dawn was insanely beautiful herself, she still didn't see it that way, even though Reuben had made her feel she was. Her self-image was damaged, just like the rest of her, but not without reason. The wolf still remained distant, while refusing to back off. He growled under his breath, and divulged his powerful fangs to her. Dawn slowly knelt down on the ground, to meet him at his level. Stretching her hand out towards him, she offered him half of the rose pedals. When the wolf didn't respond, she used her other hand to bring the rest of the rose pieces up to her lips. One by one, she placed the crimson pedals on her tongue. The wolf whimpered and tilted his head to the side, unsure what she was doing or why she was doing it. She continued to slowly chew and swallow the rose pedals as if they were *Joray Fruit Rolls*, until the only ones that remained were in the open palm of her other hand, which still reached out to him. Just as she was ready to give up and quit trying to befriend the wolf, he obediently yet cautiously walked up to her.

"There you go, baby," she said, as the wolf licked her hand, eating what was left of the rose pedals.

Convinced that she had succeeded in gaining the wolf's trust, she motioned to pet the wolf on his soft head and stroke his snowy coat. As her hand got no more than an inch from his fur, he turned and sprinted off, disappearing to what she assumed to be his eventual hibernation.

***

Three days later, the wolf tracks Dawn and begins to follow her around, refusing to leave her side. It's as if the wolf's natural instinct was to repay his debt to her, for rescuing him from the shackles of cruelty. Either that, or he was just tired of being alone and was hungry for friendship. Though she was pleased to learn that they had made a connection after all, she had thought twice about it and decided that he would be safer without her. Dawn tries to get the wolf to roam, telling him that he's *free* and *needs to find a place to call home*, but what she didn't realize was...he already had.

JANUARY 11, 1978
ESBAT
WOLF MOON

Dawn decided to name the timber wolf, *Wolf*, as she couldn't think of a better name. Wolf seemed to like it, even though it was basically simple and lacked creativity. The more time they spent together, the more they felt a kinship between them. Wolf could sense that she was one of his own, and could see the inner wolf developing inside of her. He quickly became co-dependent on her companionship, and she felt the same towards him. He wasn't a pet, but a friend…a true friend. Food was scarce, but at least they now had each other to fill their longing for family. It didn't take long before they habitually rough-housed, where she would do things like aggressively rub his stomach, and he would breathe heavily through his open mouth and occasionally bite her, playfully. Dawn would even have a dream or two, where she would strip down, pump her ass with a baby bottle, and then, while on all fours, have Wolf lap the milk as she pushed the enema out of her butthole. Then, she had another time where she dreamed that she stuck a silver butt plug in her anal cavity, which had a faux 25" fur tail attached to it. She'd run and romp on all fours, with this in her butt, chasing Wolf around in circles. Dawn, however, would never act on these frisky, subconscious thoughts of bestiality.

Agent Shelling is questioning the female sociopath, at the local police station. He had flown to New Mexico, once he heard about Heather's wild story.

"She stole my goddamn husband," Heather told him, as crocodile tears streamed down her face, which were just as counterfeit as the piecrust promises that she had made at the altar, all six times to all six husbands.

"I thought you just said that Mark beat you?" Agent Shelling asked, seeing through her narcissistic performance and not falling for her premeditated act. "Didn't you just sit there and tell me he was abusive? Why would you care if he left you for her, if he routinely beat you?"

Heather didn't acknowledge his question or show him the common courtesy of a response, but just sat there and looked at him in silent treatment. She had learned from ritualistically abusing her exes, that it stung them much deeper if she simply ignored, when men asked her anything…especially when it mattered or was important. Heather didn't feel any mortification or self-reproach for what she was. This was the same girl who was known for stealing and hiding her husband's mail, then convincing him that the Post Office was the negligent culprit. She would bribe her kids to talk quietly around her husband, just because she thought it funny that he was hard of hearing. Heather would share her food stamps with her husband and help him cut coupons, while secretly robbing him blind through all sorts of bank fraud and identity theft. She would cook for her husbands, just so she could sneak in some of her own urine into the recipe. Heather would donate her time and energy to contributing to charities and ministries, just so she could continue to keep certain people in the dark about her true nature. This was not a good person. Nothing bad ever happened to her, and nobody ever left her, which only made her feel invincible and unstoppable. So, her refusal to cooperate with the Agent's interrogation, wasn't a reflection of her nonexistent guilt, but rather poured sugar on her satisfying enmity.

Agent Shelling felt incredibly uncomfortable just sitting across from Heather. She was very quick and slick, and had a face that was much sweeter than the sinister slime that flowed through her black veins. She was like the snow, beautiful but cold. He wondered how many poor souls this gloating scourge had manipulated and destroyed, and worried about how her children would turn out…as a result of being her children. If he hadn't been such a seasoned veteran of the war called, *love*, he might have also been duped by Heather's faux charisma. What terrified him most about Heather wasn't the evil that she was capable of, but the pleasure she received from striking down those who had done

71

nothing but trust and adore her. She had no regard for human life or appreciation for love, and was more than content with conniving and scheming as many men as possible, especially when it led to a lucrative profit for her.

"So, this girl that you have described and identified as our Dawn…" Agent Shelling began, after clearing his throat, "did she actually do anything to threaten you or Mark, or put either of you in harm's way?" As badly as he craved to see Dawn's decapitated head on a platter, somehow he highly doubted that she was the monster in this particular situation.

"She ripped off the hood of our truck, with her bare hands," Heather answered. "Then, she threw it up in the air, like it was a goddamn *Frisbee*. Sorry, I didn't mean to swear. I'm a Born-Again Christian. I don't usually talk like that."

"Ah hah," the FBI Agent said, as he bobbed his head in a nod, while faking a closed-lip half-smile, "I see." He could tell that this pathological liar wasn't a credible witness, and that her simulated testimony had done nothing except make him more misogynistic and snuff a few of his brain cells. He started to find an excuse to suppress Dawn, but the impulses he saw in Heather's hollow eyes…terrified him in ways that Dawn never could.

"I'm serious," Heather insisted, "not only did she survive unscathed after colliding with our truck, but she has superhuman strength!" As Heather proceeded to press the issue, she could see that the Fed didn't believe her. Agent Shelling couldn't tell if she had a mania for madness, or if she was just having fun at his expense.

"Mrs. Campbell," he began...

"I'm not lying!" Heather rudely interrupted. "If I was lying to you, I'd also be lying to myself! Why would I want to lie to myself?" Heather proposed, trying to mess with his head, the way she had so many men before.

"I'm sorry...what?" Agent Shelling asked, completely flabbergasted by this manipulative bitch.

"I'm not lying to you! I can prove it!"

"Really? Fine, then...prove it," he challenged, knowing she was full of shit and wouldn't deliver.

Heather just sat there for several minutes, giving him silent treatment. "She stole my fucking husband!" Heather blurted, shouting louder this time. "She's a slut! A bad news, white trash, gold-digging whore!" she yelled, as her ample, yet sagged, boobs jiggled in her shamelessly...and excessively...revealing blouse.

Agent Shelling bit his tongue, as he fought the urge to emphasize that her slander was like the pot calling the kettle black, but he was significantly scared of her by this point. There was nothing admirable or praiseworthy about this chunky and conceited blonde, but to the untrained eye, he could see how men could trip over her elaborate traps. Heather was exceptional in the dark art of malice and fraud, and had mastered the malignant skill of killing others with her pseudo love. The hardened FBI agent had seen many unspeakable horrors in his time, but none of them had lived up to this rabid demon disguised in a human package.

MARCH 1, 1978
ST EICHATADT DAY
MATRONALIA

Dawn and Wolf casually walked alongside the Rio Grande River, while she wore burgundy-tinted sunglasses to block out some of the obstinate ultraviolet rays. What little snow the Winter brought the Texas plains, had finally melted, and the runoff from the ridges had filled the streams with rushing water. She wishes she had a photograph, article of clothing, or other memento of Reuben, knowing that much of his memory would regretfully and inevitably fade in the unmerited rule of time. The air was crisp and exhilarating, as she scrambled along the bank of the stream with her furry friend. She stared into the tumbling cascade, stripped nude, and leaned forward, sticking her head into the water with Wolf following her lead, right beside her. Wolf was attached to and codependent on Dawn, and she wouldn't have had it any other way. They drank the same water, and in some ways, shared the same soul.

Later, Dawn burns a campfire, using pine cones and pine trees, not for her benefit, but for her unselfish and steadfast concern for Wolf. Dawn had found that she could withstand the weather with little coverage or protection. She had developed a thick skin, as her werewolf traits were enhancing and evolving, to shield her as she continued to change with her fickle and volatile environment. The northern section of Texas got freakishly cold in the holiday season. However, the panhandle region was rather dry, so though it snowed, it wasn't quite as brutal as the white Winters she had become familiar with, growing up in the East Coast.

Though the sun's light is doing all it can to be as blinding and overbearing as possible, the temperature of the weather is still spitefully inclement. Sunset wasn't far away, and neither were her doting thoughts about her beloved Reuben. She could see his cherished face in the rising smoke, not knowing if it was all in her head or if it was his aura. Either way, whether she was imagining his unsightly manifestation or not, it was symptomatic of the eternal torch that she would always burn and carry for him. Though they were apart, he would never be truly dead...not to her. Wolf let out a howl and ran around the campfire, while Dawn saw the vision of her lost love, which only reassured her that she wasn't crazy. She was crazy about Reuben, which explained why she was going crazy without him, but she wasn't imagining seeing him now. That was the nightfall before, and the end of that February.

As Dawn rests her fatigued head on the lavender pillow, she begins to smell the scent of raspberry as she doses off to sleep. Soon after she drifts into unconsciousness, a third eye opens up in the center of her forehead, while she is completely unaware of it. Though she is oblivious to this third eye appearing on her forehead, she can see it on herself…in her dream. In reality, it looks like a regular eye, but in her dream, it is in the geometrical shape of a diamond. This dream is different than any she had experienced before, as she knew beyond the shadow of doubt that this was real. She saw herself walking towards the water's edge, on an otherwise deserted beach. She sat down in Indian-style, and gently shut her eyes. When she reopened them, she saw the beautiful cherry-blossom girl lying naked in a giant clamshell. Moments later, this same pink-haired lady is dancing nude on the beach. This mystery woman was considerably older than Dawn, and held a single pink rose in between her teeth. She spun around with her arms out to her sides, dancing in the water, as if in pure bliss. When, suddenly, the woman stopped and made eye contact with Dawn, at which point her jaw dropped, as did the flower…which fell into the cold ocean below.

When Dawn came to, she quickly reached for a pen and pad to jot down the details of her vivid dream. She knew herself well enough to anticipate forgetting her dream sequence, shortly after she rose from her slumber. She didn't wish to let that endgame happen this time, so she hurriedly wrote things down, while her combative mind was already doing its best to wipe that memory clean. This intense dream was surreal but crucial, and she knew deep inside that it meant something of paramount importance. There was a moment where Dawn doubted herself, and questioned if the lucid dream was prophetic or just a dream…that was until she found traces of sand in between her toes. She immediately feels her face to make sure she was still awake and still human, and frantically touches her clammy forehead to feel the third eye that isn't there.

Hours later, Dawn found herself relaxing on the leopard-pattern bed sheet, where Wolf was ardently cleaning her face with his attentive tongue. They were in a two-story house in the suburbs, where Dawn had broken into a few nights prior, after reckoning that it was empty and unattended. The family who lived there were away on a vacation cruise, which Dawn verified when she found a wall calendar hanging in the kitchen, that had the days marked off when they would be out of town. She and Wolf had finally been able to get some decent rest. These people were obviously well off, financially, as the house had every luxury and accommodation they could wish for. Dawn fell in love with the upstairs bathroom, which was spotless, spacious, and fitted with marble and granite. Wolf laid on the cool tiled floor, while Dawn lounged in the bathtub, soaking in therapeutic bubbles and wishing they could stay there indefinitely.

It's the month of Dawn's 19th year, coming up on the 24th, and her short shorts have gotten to be a bit malodorous. She had been itching around her crotch, which only further hinted to and warned her that she needed a change of duds. Before she drained the water, she peed in the tub, not wanting to defile the fancy toilet that looked to cost almost as much as the house. She also wasn't thrilled about using the green-colored *Cottonelle* on the toilet paper spindle. She stepped out of the tub, and didn't bother to keep her towel around her once she dried off. It was only Wolf after all, who had seen her in her birthday suit, and whom she was perfectly comfortable with. She walked into the master bedroom, and began to browse through the wife's wardrobe of outfits. To her pleasant surprise, the woman turned out to be fairly close to her size. She was also clearly a flower child, as all of the threads had that Hippy flair to them.

On the top shelf, in the woman's fashion supply, Dawn discovered an Apache-styled bone bead choker. It was black and white, with a hint of deep purple. The necklace was handmade, and comprised of pipe bone and plated silver beads. It also had a solitary white feather fastened to the front of it. Dawn observed the framed, 8"x10" *Olan Mills* portrait, that sat on the nightstand. Normally, she wouldn't swipe something that had such sacred value, but considering that the owner in question was a white woman, she saw no ethical immorality with rightfully claiming it for herself. As Wolf looked up at her with utter adoration, Dawn temporarily put her hair up, so she could easily attach the choker to her delicate and irresistible neck.

She still had her suede rucksack from her travels, that she was collecting and keeping souvenirs in, and now she had a matching tan, brown buckskin, fringe jacket that she had no intention of getting rid of or leaving behind. As she searched and snooped through the glamorous domicile, she only took what she felt would be beneficial for her and Wolf, when they had to move on and return to their quest of evasion. In her thorough examination of the magnificent rooms and walk-in closets, she uncovered some hidden bags of marijuana. She helped herself to this healthy stash by stuffing most of it in one of the pouches of her backpack, while rolling a little of it now, to test its quality. Shortly thereafter, she and Wolf were slacking in a misty daze, downstairs in the large living room.

There was a glass china cabinet against the wall, filled with everything from ceramic hand prints of the children to first editions of their favorite novels, along with a vintage porcelain China doll or two. Dawn slumped in the wicker rocking chair, while Wolf found comfort and contentment letting loose on a big beanbag chair that was lined with fluorescent-colored leather. Dawn felt inadequate and inferior, as she knew she would never afford such a lifestyle of success and independence. Though she was young and had her whole life ahead of her, she knew herself well enough to know that she would die an underachiever. She never had much luck with academics, and had always struggled with her ability to retain and learn. As she toked the joint she had carefully rolled, her hurts, habits, and hang-ups, magically got lost in the purple haze that had begun to kick in. She could feel everything she was seeing, and as she spoke and interacted, it was as if her voice and touch were coming from another body...as if she was beside or outside herself. She became lightheaded, and felt at complete ease, as if all of her cares and concerns, worries and fears, had floated off into a forgotten dimension.

MARCH 20, 1978
OSTARA (VERNAL EQUINOX)
THE SEED MOON

1978 would go down in history as a year where serial killers would either be stopped or birthed. February 1978 was Ted Bundy's final apprehension, and the year that necrophiliac and cannibal, Jeffrey Dahmer, began his homosexual killing spree. 1978 was also the year that Andrei Chikatilo (aka the Butcher of Rostov) began his reign of terror, by raping and butchering at least 52 women and children in Soviet Russia.

This calendar day was a time when light and dark were in balance. The weather had begun to turn to the Spring season, and nature had started to sprout green flowers and shake off the bitter Winter that had finally run its course. Dawn and Wolf had found short-term shelter in the warehouse part of a supermarket, which was owned by the nauseatingly corrupt *Walmart* corporation. The store manager was a deranged degenerate, who had a fetish for little girls who let him suckle on their toes, while he plays with and fingers his brown-eye. Like most corporate heads, he was hung like a leprechaun, so he had to do what he could to compensate for his sexual inadequacy. Dawn, as usual, had no problem drawing attention to herself, as it was impractical to avoid getting horny in her presence. In exchange for her submitting to his bizarre requests, which for once didn't involve her being penetrated or degraded, he let her and Wolf have free reign and take whatever merchandise they wanted, after the business closed each night. The only demand he made, which restricted them somewhat, was that Wolf had to be kept out of sight, during the daytime, as to not scare off the customers.

Dawn had contemplated seeking shelter in an Elementary school, but only briefly. If she had been caught, and if she had been a male, she would have automatically been accused of pedophilia tendencies or other diabolical intentions. As a safer alternative, she chose to target the retail market, where she was welcomed with open arms…as perverse and deviant as the stores were. While Dawn and Wolf stayed behind the scenes and hid in the warehouse, they just happened to be sitting in the wrong place at the right time. While not deliberately eavesdropping, they overheard the tail end of an *A-B* conversation. One of the superfluous supervisors was trying to console one of the petty cashiers, who was grieving over the recent loss of a loved one.

"Matthew 5:4 tells us, *blessed are those who mourn, for they will be comforted,*" the overpaid bimbo quoted, while only mimicking empathic humanity for the sake of appearance. Dawn simply shook her head and ground her teeth, clenching her fists and blinking heavily, as it took every ounce of self-control to refrain from contributing to the private discussion.

When the lead manager could break away, he would bring back milk, and poppy seed bagels, which Wolf surprisingly took an instant liking to. Dawn mostly stayed in the back with Wolf, but every so often walked out onto the retail floor, just to get some exercise. While she stretched her legs, her stomach turned, as she witnessed various mothers neglect their little ones. They either weren't paying attention or just being nonchalant, as their rambunctious rugrats used the shopping carts as a trampoline and threw groceries at other patrons. The age of proper parenting and healthy rearing had become a forgotten pastime, as if society had suddenly found instruction and discipline to be abuse. Dawn could smell potent odors of jasmine perfume, and noticed that many of the shoppers were wearing blends of green, violet, and orange.

She could see beneath the surface of others, when she passed people or made physical contact with them. She knew the countless wives and girlfriends who were lying to, stealing from, and cheating on their boyfriends and husbands. She knew these men were, for the most part, naive and in the dark about the monsters their lovers were; as they all saw their trophy women through rose-colored lenses. Dawn understood, now more than ever, why so many males eventually sought the warmth of prostitutes, who were sadly less cold than those who sought matrimony. She had learned that these unscrupulous cunts are the real whores, and not her *tricks*. Marriage, much like the rest of life, seemed to bring nothing but pain and havoc, which made her feel better about never having the chance to walk down the aisle with Reuben.

She could see the bright sun shining through the store's picture windows, which stirred up feelings of revulsion in her, as she was not a fan of the thriving solar radiation. While the ruthless sun contributed to and nurtured the growth of nature, she could have easily done without the Western heat, which always seemed to be measured only in extremes. Dawn brought back some roses for Wolf, and closely supervised him, to make sure he only ate the pedals and not the rest of the flower, which wasn't safe to digest. Agent Shelling was walking down the cereal isle, the same moment Dawn was in the next isle over, making her way to the backroom to see her furry, familiar friend. Agent Shelling never saw her, though they were literally feet apart, with only a merchandise wall in between them.

MAY 1, 1978
BELTANE
THE DYAD MOON

It was the day of supposed love and ecstasy, though Dawn was deprived of both. She had the adoring love of Wolf, who looked at her as a maternal substitute. She had the endless love of Reuben, her paranormal counterpart, who was now waiting patiently for her in the celestial realm. But, she had nothing to fill the void, that his premature death had left in her arms and loins. Reuben was more than enough for her, but she still longed for someone to meet her carnal needs while she was still physically alive. Dawn has a severe panic attack, where she collapses on the ground and can't breathe. She has a high tolerance for pain, except when it comes to matters of the heart. She misses Reuben terribly, and worries about how she's going to take care of Donnie when he's born. She hadn't had an ultrasound, but didn't need one to know that their child would be a boy. She just knew. She had shoplifted a special baby blanket, in anticipation for their child's arrival. Dawn was no marauder, but she did loot when necessary for survival, or now for her unborn son. She gripped at her chest, trying to pull on it, as she gasped for breath. Wolf cried and howled, as he eagerly waited for her vicious attack to run its course.

Dawn finally had long pants on again, which hugged her nicely-shaped hips, and covered her hypnotic legs that seemed to go on forever. After seeing clear visions of her late mother and feeling Reuben's aura, she believed in spirits, and not just the kind that's found from a bar stool. She may have turned into a ferocious killer, but she had simultaneously become a spiritual being, and nobody was going to take that away from her. Native Americans believe that there is a constant struggle between good and bad dreams. According to legend, the good dreams pass through the center hole to the sleeping person. The bad dreams are trapped in the web, where they perish in the light of day. Historically, dreamcatchers were hung in the tipi, or the lodge, or on a baby's cradle board. Dawn was no exception to this rule, as dreamcatchers had been with her since the beginning, whether she could remember them or not. Her face grew flushed, and her body temperature rose. She could feel her pulse race and her palms tingle. It wasn't the blessed presence of the Holy Spirit, but the supernatural connection to an energy source that coursed through her very veins. Just like the moon influences the tides, these ghosts strove to influence her.

"What has Immanuel done for you," a strange voice asked, which seemed to speak from nothingness, "other than do all that he can to hurt you?" Dawn wasn't always approached by familiar spirits. Sometimes, she was visited by malevolent ones, which appeared to find her just as easily.

Dawn reached up and held the front of her bone choker, sliding it from side to side, on her smooth neck, as if it was some magical amulet that she was using to meditate with. She felt as if she had a lunar crown of thorns on her head, which was effectively driving her down the lonely path towards insanity.

JUNE 20, 1978
LITHA (SUMMER SOLSTICE)
THE MEAD MOON

Dawn could have benefited from a bottle of St. John's Wort, had she had access to one and had she been educated on the herbal remedies of that drug. She had been battling anxiety, tiredness, loss of appetite (which wasn't a bad thing, considering what her diet primarily consisted of), and trouble sleeping. These were all symptomatic of depression, which science had concluded was treatable through natural or chemical substances, even though depression was more in the heart than the head. Life causes depression, not biology.

Dawn and Wolf are walking alongside the discontinued track, heading back to the abandoned train yard they had stumbled upon weeks ago. This was the longest day on the wheel of the year, when the sun is strongest and the earth is most fertile. It's hot as usual outside, but with Dawn's tough exterior and Wolf's natural insulation, they were miraculously comfortable and fortunately resilient to the brutal climate. The sun was finally setting, to offer some comfort by bringing the embrace of nightfall. There was a strong scent of vervain and chamomile in the air, which seemed to follow them like a shadow, that night.

They had been sleeping in one of the vintage railroad cars, which was being stored in this unmanaged and inactive lot. Her suede backpack rested on her shoulders, and her loyal companion stayed at her side. Without warning, Dawn was suddenly stricken with indescribable pain. She stopped walking, and keeled over, grabbing at her stomach with one hand, as she held herself up with the other. She was on her knees, crying in distress and screaming in the throes of anguish. Wolf instinctively rushed to her aid, nuzzling against the side of her face, and howling at the moon for help. Much like before, at the Falls Church mental health facility, nobody came or cared…including the Almighty himself.

"AAHH!" she continued to scream in agony, which pathetically fell upon deaf ears, with the sole exception of Wolf, who now ran circles around his master in complete panic and genuine consternation. "Wolf!" she cried out, "What's wrong with me?!" All Wolf could do was continue to whimper for her and howl in vain. Wolf was consumed with distress over Dawn. He absolutely adored her, and feared he was losing her to this unseen and unexpected threat.

Dawn felt a massive amount of blood flow out of her vagina and rush down her legs. Wolf saw her clothes saturate with blood, and noticed the red pool that she was making underneath her. He wanted to run away to find anyone who might be able to help her, but he couldn't bear to abandon her. He was torn on what to do, and for the first time in his life, he was terrified. Dawn was weeks away from being due, and still somehow managed to not show her pregnancy. She hadn't gained any weight, and now the baby was coming early. She convulsed violently, as if she was going to vomit, but wound up projecting blood instead of puke.

Her complexion began to turn a unique shade of lavender. She reached down to undo her rainbow bellbottoms, but was too weak and too scared to finish what she had started. These jeans had a rainbow curving up one leg, swerving around her forever-13-year-old hip, and back down the other leg. Wolf sensed that she needed to get her pants off, so he immediately secured one of her legs with his jaw and bit down just hard enough to lock her leg in his mouth. He then tugged on her leg, forcing it to straighten, which made the other leg collapse as well. Once he had Dawn lying flat on her stomach, he grabbed the bottom sleeve of her hiphuggers and pulled her pants off. Wolf then used his nose and his extra-large feet to roll her over onto her back. Dawn wasn't wearing her regular *Underoos*, which would prove to be a blessing in this particular scenario.

As Dawn screamed in futility, Wolf used the strength of his fangs to pull up on her knees, encouraging her to bend them. He naturally knew what this was, and was overwhelmed with dread, as he was perceptive enough to know that all the birth blood coming out of her was highly unusual and extremely abnormal. Dawn finally realized that she was in labor, which worried her since she had experienced no morning sickness, her water hadn't broken, and this baby was coming three weeks premature.

Screaming in unbearable torment, Dawn laid on her back, right there on the side of the railroad track, and pushed out Reuben's child. When the baby finally came out, Wolf was the first to see that something was wrong. The infant wasn't moving. Once Dawn had caught her second wind, and had brought her pulse down to a level where she could think, she noticed that their son was perfectly silent.

"Why aren't you crying?" she asked, as she used all of her strength to push herself up, so she could see her baby. The newborn laid there between her spread-eagle legs, attached to the umbilical cord. Wolf backed away a few feet, in trepidation of how Dawn would react.

Dawn scooped up her limp baby off the ground, and brought him up to her face, so she could get a better look at the death she just delivered. Dawn's body was mostly drenched in blood, as she looked at their lost baby. Dazed in denial, she pressed her free hand against his little chest, while cradling him with her other arm. She leaned over and blew air into his mouth, to no avail.

"Your heart's not beating," she said softly, knowing full well that her son couldn't hear her. "Your heart's not beating," she repeated herself, as if subconsciously trying to somehow understand the cruel nature of God. A stampede of emotions filled her thoughts, as the forsaken young woman was once again dealt loss and disappointment. She couldn't make sense out of how or why there would have been complications, since she hadn't exhibited any forewarning signs of hazard or malfunction.

She could feel her very essence being overcome by frantic despair. Every inch of Dawn's body trembled with sadness and anger. She couldn't make sense out of the fact that she had hemorrhaged all over herself, and yet her newborn had a heart that was deprived of a single drop. Dawn tried one last time, in desperation, to wake their son, but was sadly unsuccessful. She still feels no heartbeat from his tiny chest, nor movement from his face. She looked down at Donnie, with her lower lip quivering and her eyes burning with tears. He looked so much like Reuben, that the resemblance was almost uncanny. She threw her head back and yelled at God, cursing the Lord for once again taking from her that which she so cherished.

"Fuck you!!" she said, damning God for robbing her of her only son. "Why?! Why couldn't you let me have our boy?! Why is it too much to ask for some fucking empathy from you?! You cold-hearted son of a bitch!!"

Wolf, very cautiously, eased back up to her and saw that he wasn't in any danger. He slightly raised his paw and, as gently as he could, used his protruded claw to sever the cord. Dawn rocked herself back and forth like a lunatic, as if trapped in a vegetative state of mind, while Wolf stepped up…so that he was as close to them as he could be. As Dawn continued to stare aimlessly into nothingness, and be lost in the mist of madness, Wolf licked the stillborn face and then licked hers. He wanted them to know that he was there, and even though he couldn't help either of them, that his heart beat and broke for them both.

"Aww," a condescending voice said from behind, in a phony, yet syrupy accent. "What's the matter, Mummy? Why you cryin' like a little baby? Your lovely baby's died, has it?"

As it turned out, there had been a couple people nearby, who not only heard Dawn's desperate cries for help, but also stood back and callously observed the whole dreadful ordeal. Both of the heartless spectators looked as if they had either been hunting or marching. They had worn the whole get-up, everything from the leather combat boots to the surplus clothing. They dressed themselves as if they were some neo-version of the military, but it was evident that they were nothing more than Nazi wannabes. They just wore trefoil (a three-rounded clover design) instead of swastikas. The male member of the duo even had his head clean shaven, to further illustrate his supremacist colors. He spoke with a bad British accent and reeked of mugwort.

"Look, Felix, the Navajo slut can't even keep her little Injun up," his insensitive, white trash girlfriend said. "No wonder the father's not around," she mocked, adding insult to injury.

"Probably better this way, isn't it?" the vulgar skinhead agreed with his lowlife whore. "She likely doesn't even have any bloody papers."

"Are you referring to the girl or the dog?" the blonde bimbo asked her impersonator boyfriend.

"Is there a difference, mate?" the impostor laughed. "Rubbish is rubbish, isn't it?"

The despicable couple laughed at Dawn, whom they viewed as an amusing train wreck. Herein lies the irony, as they were the ones who pretended to be something they weren't, with him faking being British (and inaccurately and offensively misrepresenting them at that) ... and both of them having glaciers where their hearts should have been. This nefarious couple was one of the many scourges infecting the earth, and these human devils were finally about to get their due.

Wolf slowly turned his head around, to face the inconsiderate offenders and give them the evil eye. The pair had made the fatal error in mistaking him to be a common Siberian Husky, or some domesticated malamute. When they saw Wolf's piercing yellow eyes, they began to immediately rue their behavior. As soon as he senses that they knew he was a wolf, he could smell their fear like it was burnt coffee. Wolf snarled and growled at them, showing his razor-sharp incisors that could frighten the most hardened of criminals. They began to slowly back away, when Wolf leapt at them, knocking them both down. Within seconds, he had ripped open their throats from the windpipe to the spinal column, hence staining his taupe nail. The couple looked to be in their late twenties and had actually come with the intention of mugging Dawn in her time of confusion, and instead had their larynx torn out. They had chosen the wrong time to take advantage of Dawn, even though Wolf still would have made them pay, traumatic birth-failure or not.

Dawn laid her aching head on his warm coat of banded fur and wept herself to sleep, as her face and hands shook violently with seizure-like tremors. Wolf licked her face a bit and watched over her for a while longer, before joining her in her much-needed rest. Dawn had a dream, where she was a breakfast cereal character, who magically leapt off the sugary box and murdered everyone in the family home.

When Dawn woke the next morning, Dawn and Wolf were still nuzzling together in mutual comfort and support. Hoping that the dire devastation of the previous night had been nothing more than a wrenching nightmare, she felt the dried, crusted blood coating her body, and found her dead baby still cradled in her arms.

Her tears quickly revisited her sore eyes, but came much gentler this time. Dawn made one last futile attempt to revive the little guy from his eternal slumber by putting her mouth over his, and trying to give him CPR, knowing that her effort was in vain. She discovers something in the dirt beside her, which looks to be interesting enough to dig up. She uses her clawed fingers to dig around the small object and finally pulls it out of the ground. As she looks at it, she doesn't identify or recognize what it is, but it turns out to be an XX rune stone.

"Hmm, interesting rock," she says out loud to herself, before tossing it over her left shoulder like a pinch of salt. Dawn sets her cherished child down beside her, and turns and looks at her hairy friend. Wolf gently bats his eyes at her, as he releases a soft whimper. Dawn's trampled heart is soothed as much as it can be by her friend's genuine and unspoken sentiment. "I love you too," she tells him. "Why don't we have some breakfast, unalii."

They get up off the ground and walk over to the two slaughtered bodies that Wolf had dismembered. Flies buzzed around the fresh corpses, and the stank was already rancid. They both simultaneously dined from the bodies, devouring their internal organs, as if they had developed a taste for raw and putrid meat. They gorged themselves, but not to excess. They only fed to the degree of sustaining them for the next couple days or so.

Leaving the carcasses there, Dawn picks up her deceased baby, and she and Wolf continue to walk to the deserted rail yard.

On their way there, they come to a *Cavender's* western-wear store. They veer off their route, to take care of what needs to be done. Stepping into the retail outlet, the employees and customers stop what they're doing and collectively gawk at the terrifying duo. Dawn looked like Sissy Spacek did in, *Carrie*, while Wolf made sure that everyone remained subdued and subjugated. Ranchers and poachers stared at the conspicuous pair, torn on how to react. Everyone in the boutique was scared shitless at the sight of them. Dawn was still holding her dead newborn, whom everyone could clearly see, which only made her and Wolf even more frightening to the shoppers and staff. Wolf cautiously follows Dawn up to the checkout counter.

"I need a change of clothes, private use of your washroom, a lighter, and a gallon container of gasoline," Dawn communicated, in a calm yet demanding voice.

"Um, we're a family clothing store," the female clerk told her. "We can set you up with a change of clothes and give you private use of our facilities, but we can't help you with your other requests," the woman told her, trying to hide that she was shaking like a leaf in the wind.

"I have a gas can in my truck," one of the male customers volunteered. "I can help her."

Wolf noticed that a more conventional family was trying to sneak slowly towards the exit, and quickly ran back to guard the doors.

"I'm sorry," Dawn apologized, "but nobody can leave until my wolf and I are ready to leave. We're not here to harm anyone. We just need your help with a few things, and then we'll be on our way and out of yours." Everyone seemed to be happy to comply, either with an agreeing nod or by holding their peace. "Thank you, sir," she said, turning to make eye contact with the elderly man with the truck. "I appreciate your kind generosity." Dawn started to make her way towards the young women's section of the store, to find a fresh outfit, when it occurred to her that she was still holding her stillborn child. She turned back around one more time, and walked up to the counter to address the lady cashier. "I hate to bother you again," she said, as she laid her child down on the counter, "but could you watch my baby and maybe put him in a box for me? I need something I can carry him in, when Wolf and I are finally ready to get out of your hair."

"Sure," the woman agreed without dispute or debate, as she pissed her pants, completely in shock.

"Thank you again," Dawn showed appreciation, as she went browsing through the store. Everyone remained frozen in fear, while Wolf stayed by the door to keep people from leaving or entering.

Once Dawn had cleaned herself up and taken enough to replenish what needed to be discarded, she was ready to leave the establishment. While she had read about detestable mothers dumping their babies in public garbage receptacles, she wasn't about to disgrace or desert her child that way. Besides, those mothers were cruel and unfeeling, doing that to their babies whether they were alive or dead. None of this changed the fact, however, that she had a stillborn son that she couldn't bring back, regardless of how desperately she wanted to keep and resurrect him. She was faced with the unwanted task of disposing his remains, which she could either do by burial or cremation. Though it shattered her heart to do so, she decided on the latter option, as it would take less time and be more efficient in not leaving any evidence for the police to find later. Donnie's corpse would only leave DNA for the cops to trace back to her. She couldn't let that happen, as much as it destroyed her to say goodbye to Reuben's son.

Dawn did not want to do this, and it began to show in her somatic demeanor. Wolf looked up at her out of alarm, sensing that she was acutely distraught. When she looked back down at Wolf, and locked eyes with his, she took on a whole other layer of psychosis. Though Wolf hadn't imparted this at all, she heard a distinct voice come from him that no one else could hear. She, in her unstable and unhinged state of delusion, believed she heard Wolf tell her not to leave any loose ends. The voice, that she was confident she heard, was not in animal dialect but in fluent English.

"Toss me your keys," she said to the old man who had offered to help her out with the gasoline. She could see the doubt and worry in his eyes, as he had expected to be able to walk out with her and get it for her. "I'll throw you your keys back, I promise." The helpful senior distrusted her, but he knew that he had no choice. Linda was there, as always, showing up to wail just before Dawn did her thing.

Dawn and Wolf walk out alone, leaving little Donnie inside with the dismayed cashier. While Dawn tends to the pickup, Wolf faces the doors to the store, making sure none of the patrons or personnel escape. Though it's the hardest thing for Dawn to do, she burns the infant's body in the Western boutique, along with everyone else. Dawn holds the doors shut, with her bare hands this time, while she once again commits arson. As the place burns to the ground, they can hear the deafening screams coming from inside. Some of the victims forcefully push and pull on the doors, only to find they were no match for Dawn's strength or stamina. A few others bust through the window and try to make a run for it, only to be met with Wolf's matchless agility and unrivaled aggression.

After the deed is done and everyone had perished, besides her and Wolf, Dawn honors her vow and throws the man's keys into the blazing building. She could have taken the truck, but had enough prudence to know that it would only bring trouble. Dawn then collapses on the ground. Grabbing at the center of her chest, she falls apart and has another severe panic attack that feels more like a cardiac arrest. Her heart is pounding, her spine is tingling, and her vision blurring. This one was as afflicting as the last one, but because she now knew what to expect, she could better handle the agony. This unbearable trauma brings Dawn and Wolf closer together, but also hardens her heart more than it was already. Dawn had been carrying around the baby blanket that she had shoplifted earlier, for little Donnie's arrival. It has a wolf pattern on it, blended with different pastel colors. Though their son was dead, she couldn't bring herself to get rid of the unused blanket, so she added it to the contents of her rucksack.

Dawn and Wolf spend hours that night, hugging and sobbing together in mourning. Dawn considered those people a burnt offering to the phlegmatic God, whom she saw more and more as a sociopath. From then on, she thinks that Wolf is telepathically telling her who to kill…as well as when and why. Only Dawn's warped mind can hear him speak to her, and now Wolf's alleged encouragement is at odds with Linda's persistent dissuasion. Though this was merely symptomatic of her progressive meltdown and Wolf wasn't actually directing Dawn in her warpath, Dawn had picked up on something else that wasn't at all a psychotic delusion.

Wolf could see Linda's ghost when she would show up to wail at her deteriorating daughter, just before Dawn would take a life. As Dawn held Wolf close, cradling him in her arms, he buried his cold nose into her warm bosom. Wolf kept watchful guard, snarling at anyone who dared as much as look at them wrong.

SEPTEMBER 16, 1978
LUNAR ECLIPSE

Dawn cuts herself with a fillet knife that she found in the dirty kitchen, slicing her arms deep enough to draw blood and leave scars, but not enough to sever a major artery. She's sitting on the neglected floor, in the corner of the cabinets, while the water pours out of the faucet in the sink above. Wolf, of course, licks her wounds clean, even as she makes them. He hates seeing her like this, but is wise enough to know that there is nothing he can do to stop her quest of self-destruction. He only hopes that his loyalty and friendship will be reason enough for her to slow down the process some. The Deep Purple hit, *Smoke On The Water*, is playing on a radio that's plugged into the wall. The wall looks like an electrical hazard, the radio is covered in cobwebs, and the hot steam is turning into a black mist.

The one positive side to Dawn's persistent self-mutilation, was that the werewolf in her made her immune system like none other. So, even carelessly using a rusty blade on her own flesh, which was considerably unhygienic, she was no longer prone or powerless to the myriad of diseases that others needed to guard themselves against. Dawn was by no means invincible, but she had become exceptionally resilient. She would, on the other hand, never get used to or grow numb to, the pain that had taken up permanent residence in her broken heart. They say that *time heals all wounds*, but it only teaches how to live with them, if you can survive at all. Those who claim that *what doesn't kill you makes you stronger*, have never known real tragedy or suffered the way Dawn had. Anyone who could believe such nonsense, had clearly never been backstabbed by life or let down by God.

That night, Dawn had fallen asleep spooning with Wolf, in the old, ramshackle house, which from the looks of it had clearly been relinquished long ago. This place was off by itself, in the middle of the woods, miles from any neighbor or business. Dawn had found some dusty blankets that she shook off on the porch, and brought back inside to construct a makeshift tipi for them to sleep under, while they laid together on the floor. As Dawn snuggled with Wolf from behind, wrapping her left arm around his neck, she spoke softly to Reuben as if he was actually there with them. About nine minutes before she completely fell asleep, she began to dream…while she was still awake…which would carry on and continue in her slumber. A lunar eclipse was taking place in the night sky, which completely escaped Dawn's attention, as she was too focused and burned-out to notice.

In Dawn's dreams, she was as deadpan as she was in reality. Her personality was a reflection of her lament. This dream would be different, as it would revisit the fair-haired fox that she had seen before. Her dream launched with a wolf running through the wilderness. This wolf wasn't the frosted, lovable companion she had come to befriend, but felt like a literal double of herself. This wolf was dirt-brown, had sky-blue eyes, and was undoubtedly female. Dawn couldn't tell if she was running from or towards something. She felt connected to this wolf, in a way that she couldn't share with Wolf. It was as if this dark wolf was a mirror-image of her own soul. The wolf, as an animal totem, is fiercely loyal and true, yet usually retains its freedom and independence. The wolf is also often associated with the psychic aspects of lunar lore.

As the brown wolf ran voraciously through the remote forest, Dawn could feel her feelings and see through her eyes. Just as they merged into one blended spirit, she saw the rosy-haired stranger again. This time, the mysterious beauty was standing in a clearing, which was encircled by towering trees. She was alone, bare naked, and held her arms up to the heavens, as if looking up in solemn prayer. Her hands began to glow with this blinding white energy, which quickly spread over and engulfed her entire body. Her *Kool-Aid*-treated hair began to flow back behind her, as if she was facing a storm that wasn't there.

As the wolf continued to frenetically run towards this enchanting woman, she leapt up into the air, once she got close enough. As the brown wolf was in mid-leap, she turned from animal-form to Dawn, who was also stark naked. Landing on the pink-haired mystic, she knocked the woman over, and before she knew it, they were enthralled in the throes of uninhibited passion. While they were engaged in a heated embrace, going at it as if there was no tomorrow, Dawn noticed the woman's eyes, which radiated an engrossing oceanic shade. Before Dawn knew what she had dove into, this intimate stranger was draining her life force and not letting her go until she fed on Dawn's very soul. She sucked on her, both bodily and spiritually, as Dawn could feel herself losing control and getting lost in this woman's affections.

SEPTEMBER 21, 1978
MABON
HARVEST MOON

The turncoat trio are browsing the local head shop, which sells a wide variety of natural and metaphysical supplies. Joy carefully looked at the different herbs on the many shelves. Certain ones like marigold, sunflowers, hibiscus, roses, and myrrh, were luckily marked down in price. Maria was busy checking out the selection of sterling silver rings, each of which had a specific stone on the top; such as amber, tiger-eye, and citrine. The management had come to dread these three girls, so much that they let them take whatever they wanted, fearful that any attempt to upset or apprehend them would only lead to eternal retaliation.

"The great Sun had awoken," Bonnie said, while stuffing her mouth with a handful of purple grapes that she hadn't paid for. "Let's go to church," she suggested, while standing in the produce section of the elaborate and eclectic store. Joy and Maria both turned their heads to gander at their grazing friend, and smirked with her in one accord. "It's the Autumn Equinox. We should go celebrate," she suggested, hoping that Joy would agree.

Despite her better judgment, Dawn makes a valiant effort one last time, to reach out to the Nazarene Lord. Though she's pretty certain, at this point, that God hates her, it didn't change or remove the fact that she was terrified of the idea of burning in Hell. The tormented half-Cherokee enters the tainted church, with her head hanging low, seeking temporary sanctuary from the growing blue-heat outside. As Dawn sat in the back row of the church, listening intently to the fundamental service. she continues to get nasty looks from the other parishioners for having brought in a wolf with her. In spite this shunning abhorrence and detesting judgment, Wolf calmly sits at the end of the pew next to Dawn, like a well-trained domesticated pup, not making a sound or a scene.

"Acts 7:42 tells us that God turned his back to them, and gave them up to the worship of the sun and the moon. The Gospel warns us about idolatry in Exodus 20:3&5, 34:14, and what the harsh consequences are in Deuteronomy 6:15. He tells us in John 14:6 that no one will be allowed entrance into paradise, unless they treat Jesus as the only true God. Then, in John 6:44, we are told that Jesus won't allow the dead into Heaven until the day of his second coming, which means that all of our deceased loved ones are neither in Heaven nor Hell, but waiting patiently in the darkness of the ground, for God knows how long," he preaches, doing what every minister does, as he misinterprets the Bible and misrepresents God.

As Dawn tries earnestly to listen to the mountebank at the pulpit, she is distracted by three young women who are sitting on the pew across from her, to her left. They look to range between eighteen and twenty-two, and are all dressed in matching, vibrant, yellow, hooded sweat jackets. They're giggling, and staring at her and Wolf, making Dawn feel awkwardly uncomfortable.

"She's a shaman," Bonnie whispered to Joy. Bonnie had short hair with long bangs, that was straight but curled inward at the ends, which covered her ears and forehead; as opposed to Joy and Maria, who both had long, straight hair.

They clearly weren't listening to the sermon, which quickly resumed to the pastor preaching about false gods, not having other gods before Jehovah, and witchcraft being a forbidden abomination. Halfway through the Sunday morning service, the three child-like women get up and come over to sit next to Dawn. Again, Wolf remains completely calm and unthreatening.

"We love your familiar," the green-eyed Maria whispered in Dawn's ear.

"My what?" Dawn asked, softly, as to not disturb the congregation.

"Your pet," Joy clarified, in layman's terms.

"He's not my pet," she whispered back. "He's my friend."

Overhearing this, Wolf whimpered, and licked his mouth as he looked up at Dawn, whom he couldn't have adored more. Though Dawn is a little freaked out by these girls, she begins to feel strangely relaxed, as she breathes in the jasmine-scented aroma coming from the three young women. Her strong sense of smell can also detect a hint of lavender, coming from their shared perfume.

"Don't leave after the service," Joy authoritatively requested. "We want a chance to chat with you." Dawn bowed her head, not to nod in agreement, but to notice Joy's hand boldly resting on her inner thigh. Dawn would have normally brushed the hand off in protest, but she was hypnotized and captivated by Joy's many rings on her left hand. She had one on every finger, which each held a different gemstone.

"The seven deadly sins," the pastor continued his unconventional yet Biblically supported sermon, "are allegedly lust, gluttony, greed, sloth, wrath, envy, and pride. This is what we're told. This, however, is not Scriptural. Nowhere in the Bible does it refer to seven deadly sins. In fact, the Bible clearly states that all sin is considered equal and forgiven, in God's eyes…well, that is, unless you blaspheme his Holy Spirit. Mark 7:21-23 says that adultery, theft, murder, envy, fraud, malice, pride and stupidity are the eight deadly sins. Then, Proverbs 6:16-19 professes that there are six deadly sins, which are lust, deceit, murder, malice, embracing evil, and cruel intentions. So, the Bible, as usual, is all over the map on its claims."

When the service had wrapped, and the congregation was dispersing and returning to their cars to go their separate ways, the three young women made their way outside to patiently wait for Dawn to follow in their shadow. Dawn had already chosen to not rush to leave the sanctuary, as she wanted to give orthodox Christianity one last chance before entirely sweeping that faith under the rug.

"Excuse me, pastor," she called out, "can I have an audience with you for a moment?"

The pastor graciously agreed and sat down alongside Dawn, at the end of one of the first pews, closest to the pious stage. Wolf, once again sat in silence, but kept a close eye on their surroundings, as he didn't trust anyone but Dawn. Wolf was perceptive enough to tell that there was something off with this minister, but as long as the priest wasn't an immediate threat to her, he didn't care enough to attack the man. Wolf picked his battles, and didn't lunge at someone purely because they were a fraud. If he did, he wouldn't have any time to breathe, since he'd have to go after most of mankind. Dawn kept much of the details private, but summarized her plagued life in a brusque, yet informative, disclose. She was looking for consolation from this perfidious and fickle evangelist, hoping that he might somehow find a way to reinvigorate the shred of faith that she once felt…or at least wanted to feel.

"It's killing me, because if I stop believing in God, then I can't likely expect to see my Reuben and our baby in Heaven…and that is a thought that is just too painful to swallow," she said, while fighting back the flow of tears that struggled to float to the surface.

"Bless your heart," he told the distressed Dawn. "You are so sweet, but so naive. The Bible tells us, in Matthew 18:18, that whatever we lose on earth, will still be lost in Heaven. Christians like to delude themselves in buying this fairy tale that God is benevolent enough to let us reconcile, reunite, and reconnect with our loved ones in the afterlife. But, according to the Gospel, if you really study it, God isn't nearly that romantic or empathetic," he told her, deliberately crushing her dreams and hopes, taking twisted delight in murdering what was left of her to snuff.

Dawn holds her ears like a severe autistic, pressing her palms against the sides of her throbbing and troubled head. She squints her eyes hard, as if trying to force her own thoughts out of her disturbed mind. She had needed comforting reassurance, but instead got religious regurgitation. She hated what the perverse preacher was saying to her, but had little to no doubt that he was telling the truth. She wanted to trust that the Bible's words were more loving than that, but she had suffered enough rude awakenings and wake-up calls to know differently.

"My head hurts," she told him, while really talking about her heart.

"Sometimes, the mind is a terrible thing," he reaffirmed. "Matthew 10:16 says, *behold, I send you out as sheep amongst the wolves*," the radical preacher says to Dawn. "Psalm 90:10 then goes onto say that, *the best of our days are promised to bring us toil, trouble, and sorrow, and then we die*. This is the loving God that is in the Bible; a God who deliberately puts us in the path of danger, sets out to fill our lives with pain, and then tops it all off with a bitter slice of death. I believe in God. I do. If I didn't, I wouldn't be a man of the cloth. But, don't be fooled into buying this Judeo-Christian propaganda that God is kind. There are plenty examples in the Bible that point to the contrary, and all you really have to do is look at the Christian church to find ruthlessness and hatred."

"No offense," Dawn began, "but, you really don't strike me as being God-friendly."

"No offense taken," he confessed, "and you're partially right."

"Then why are you a fundamentalist preacher at all?" she asked him. "Why the charade?"

"I believe in God, but I'm not naive or disillusioned. I don't set out to trick my sheep, or pretend that God is something he's not. This world is cruel, and the Messiah is no different. I do what I do, because it's important to me to be a spokesperson of the truth…the *real* truth."

"Aren't you afraid you'll burn in Hell for saying that?" she questioned.

"John 11:26 tells us that all we have to do is believe in him, and we will never perish. As I said, I believe in God. I just know he's a prick. Most Americans think that our founding fathers were Christians, but that's simply not the case. Ben Franklin, for example, was a member of *The Hellfire Club*, and considered himself a Satanist. When he first discovered electricity, and began to show the extent of its benefits and capabilities, people thought he was a witch. Ironically enough, Ben's mother was one of the women who was initially accused of witchcraft, just before the biased Salem Witch Trials of 1692. She just happened to convince them otherwise, at the last minute, before the other twenty were unjustly murdered."

Dawn suppressed the darker side of her personality, resisting the tempting opportunity to take out this execrable example of Modern-American Christianity.

"Hang in there," the knockoff clergyman advised, while he cringes around Wolf, who is staring up at him with deadly silence. "Remember what Jeremiah 29:11 promises us. God has a plan to prosper you and not harm you, and to give you hope and a future. Hang in there."

Dawn thanked the contradictory minister for his time in hearing her out, then walked down the center isle to the exit doors. As Dawn and Wolf stepped into the blinding daylight, she was quickly pulled aside. Her conversation with the eerie trinity would continue right there, on the left side of the brick-and-mortar house of the Savior.

"Merry meet," Joy said to Dawn.

"Namaste," Dawn said in return, confused on how to interpret these human oddities, but nonetheless making an effort to be well-mannered and respectful.

They proceeded to tell Dawn that they are members of a coven called, *The Golden Veil*, which worship the ancient horned god, Osiris, and the moon goddess, Isis, and is run by a glorified guru whom they call, *The Beast*. They spoke about this, as if their secret club was completely normal and common. There were no signs of shame or suspicion on any of the three girls' faces. To them, this Satanic coven was a regular and acceptable affiliation.

"But you're Christians?" Dawn said, confused. "You're at a Christian church."

"No, no," Bonnie told her. "We only come here, on occasion, for a witch hunt."

"Yeah," Maria corroborated. "We're just here on a witch hunt."

The one who seemed to be their spokesperson, perceived that they were only further confusing Dawn. "We don't mean, *witch hunt*, as in looking for those to burn at the stake," Joy clarified. "We use the term to describe how we visit churches, like this one, and look for those whom we feel are doubting their faith or scoffing at what the preacher is teaching. We look for those who are lonely, bitter, damaged, or angry, and seduce them with carnal temptations like sex or drugs. That's when we intervene and snatch the person away from Jehovah, bringing them into our sacred Circle."

"I see," Dawn said. "So, what do you want with me? Do I seem weak to you?" she asked their leader, as she and Wolf smiled at each other through eye contact.

"No," Joy answered, who was a few years Dawn's elder. "Not at all. Just the opposite, in fact. Isis, our goddess, is an ancient symbol of Luna," she began, while showing Dawn the eerie, pewter amulet hanging from the chain around her neck, which was carved in the shape of a crescent moon that cradled a small five-pointed star. "She is also a symbol of transformation."

"I don't understand?" Dawn said, playing dumb to protect herself.

"I think you do," Joy told her. "We can see you for what you are," she said, "and we approve. We think you're divine, and want you to join our Circle." Joy really just wanted Dawn for the power she could bring to the table, not her as a person. She slipped Dawn a folded piece of paper that had a coded message on it, which was basically regular English written backwards. It gave directions on how to get to a Moon Lodge, where they were currently retreating.

"You should come," the three girls told Dawn, in unison, which further creeped her out.

"Seriously," Joy reiterated, "you should come. Your wolf is welcome to," she offered, subtly inviting both her pet and her inner demon.

"I don't even know what a Moon Lodge is," Dawn confessed.

"All you need to know is that it's a place where there is no inhibition or repression, just indulgence and relaxation," Joy explained. "The moon is a symbol of the unconscious, where the Divine dwells…and the lodge represents relief from the stress, interruption, and responsibilities of daily life."

"The moon is a portal to our subconscious and a mirror to our instincts, intuitions, and deepest emotions," Bonnie added.

"The sun gives you carcinoma," Maria further educated, "while the moon offers nothing but comfort and power. Even the tides of the ocean, and of our womb, listen to its' wisdom. Farmers plant and harvest according to the lunar phases," Maria elaborated, speaking of the moon as if it were God himself.

Dawn looked down and noticed that all three girls had identical tattoos on the web of their left hands. Joy perceived this, and responded by raising her limp wrist to Dawn, as if believing herself to be a regal princess who expected the back of her hand to be kissed. Dawn took her hand into her own, and leaned over to get a closer look at the intricate tattoo, which possessed a rune-like design.

"It's called the *Seal of Babylon*," Joy educated her, while reading her mind. The tattoo was a seven-pointed star, known as the *Septogram*, originally coined by the late Satan worshipper, Aleister Crowley. "Babylon is considered to be the mother of abominations, or the great harlot," Joy proudly added.

"You can be a whore too," Maria told Dawn, just as boastfully, as she came up from behind and wrapped her arms around Joy's neck.

"You should come to the Moon Lodge," Bonnie repeated. "You could have a tattoo like this too. Come be with us, and meet Vaingory."

"Yes," Joy agreed, grinning at Dawn, while gently biting the tip of her forefinger and subtly twisting her hips. "Master Vaingory would go absolutely crazy for you."

"You should come," Maria said.

"Yes," Joy again agreed. "You should come."

She was torn between seeing these vixens as coyotes and giving these tricksters the benefit of the doubt. "Thank you for the kind invite," Dawn politely appreciated. "I will consider it."

Joy, Maria, and Bonnie all embraced Dawn with warm hugs, and even showed Wolf some love, who surprisingly let them. They said their farewells and left Dawn to consider their offer, which of course she never did. She did feel forsaken by Jehovah, and the girls had picked up on that vibe, but Dawn was no candidate for recruitment. She was vulnerable, but not impressionable. She longed to belong, but was too strong to be gullible and too sharp to be someone's prey. Once Dawn and Wolf were out of sight, the three witches hold hands and chant.

"By the power of three, let her see, that we are the only place to be." They repeated this prayer three times, with their eyes closed as if in deep meditation. They did this as a precaution, just in case Dawn chose not to take them up on their invite to the exclusive spa resort.

Agent Shelling has commissioned a Catholic priest to consecrate a special bullet. As he patiently waited there at the church, for the collared clergyman to fulfill his request, the FBI crusader was distracted with an emotional call. He received a distressing message on his pager, which demanded his prompt response. Stepping outside the church, he was overwrought with the immediate need to find a pay phone, which he spotted across the street, at a gas station. Moments later, he found himself on the phone with William's mother. His sister was inconsolable, having just gotten word from her doctor that she had been diagnosed with a brain aneurism that was both positioned and shaped in a way, which made it impossible to treat or correct with surgery.

"I will track her," he swore to his tortured sister. "I will bring the bitch to justice. William will be avenged. I will make sure she serves a life sentence, without parole, in a maximum security prison," he carelessly pledged to the victim's mother, lying through his teeth, while having every intention of putting Dawn in the ground himself.

The noctivagant drifter and her trusty companion happened upon a hidden lake, which was a well-kept secret in old El Paso. This was a body of water which was nestled between I-10 and Loop 375. This *Portland Cement Reservoir* wasn't anything compared to the *Trail of the Rio Grande*, but it sufficed in serving its purpose. After they paused to quench their hydration, Dawn washed her hair in the waterhole, while Wolf romped in the refreshing pool. On their way back to the road, Dawn kneeled down to suck up some drops of liquid nourishment from one of Wolf's paw-prints. The magnificent white wolf was soaked in the earth's tears, and had left his mark in the soil...as well as in Dawn's heart. Dawn recalled one of the countless sermons she grew up listening to. She remembered her father preaching on Jeremiah 17:9, which states that *the heart is wicked and deceitful*, to the degree that we can't know it...but this is one of those exceptional Bible verses that are entirely false and evidently contributed by man, not God. A heart is only wicked if its owner is heartless.

Dawn knew her heart better than anyone, and there was nothing deceptive about it.

The scantily clad Dawn continued doing whatever was necessary to not only keep herself going, but more importantly, to make sure that Wolf was properly cared for. God may have taken Reuben's boy away from her, but she wasn't going to let him take her Wolf away. She had no morals or limits anymore, and was capable of just about anything, but the difference between her and women like Heather was that she didn't enjoy it. Dawn had become a monster, but it was a monster that brought her shame and remorse. She would occasionally have nightmares, where Wolf would wake up to find her screaming or weeping in her sleep. She didn't get off on hurting others, but only did it for survival. Dawn wasn't heartless, but actually died a little more inside every time she took a life. She, however, couldn't deny that she did find pleasure and satisfaction in killing those who were unquestionably and inherently wicked. In this case, each and every time she got to rid the planet of another one, it got easier and more fun.

OCTOBER 16, 1978
SOLAR ECLIPSE
HUNTER'S MOON

They eventually found themselves in the college town of Midland, where a gothic carnival was in progress. Dawn arrived at the fiesta early, before it was open to the public. She passed a few hotrods that caught her eye, like the candy apple, 1970 AMC *Javelin*, and the yellow and black 1970 Plymouth AAR *Cuda* 340. She casually walked in, without any objection, or anyone demanding that she have a ticket, mainly because of her intimidating look and fierce companion. No one looked at Wolf with disdain or distemper, since they were in an environment that welcomed the macabre and mysterious. However, though Dawn and Wolf fit well and blended in, the carnies were also wise enough not to fuck with them. As Dawn wandered and browsed through the sensational experience of the dark circus, she came upon a sideshow. As she began to step through the curtains to enter the eerie attraction, a midget approached her. The little person introduced himself as, *Imp*.

"I'm actually a regular dwarf," he clarified. "It just makes me look more special, if I go by the mythological label."

Imp took it upon himself to be Dawn's guide through the covered spectacle of the obscene and obscure. She was repulsed as he showed her these outcasts, all locked away in captivity, while they waited to be called upon for their next demeaning performance. These weren't monsters, but human beings who had just been dealt a shitty hand, which Dawn could certainly relate. These freaks each had a steel cage, with a metal name tag on the bottom of their bars, identifying them by their character name. Imp explained their personas and conditions, as they came up to each one.

"This is Elven," he told her. "His ears are naturally pointed. He was born with a genetic malformation, which mutated the placement and shape of his external ears."

Dawn saw that Elven was crouching in the corner, showing Dawn his profile of sadness. He was naked from the waist up, and she could see many linear scars on his arms. He wore green tights which were patterned and designed to look like leaves.

"Why does he look all cut up?" she asked Imp.

"They used to let him have a bow and arrow, to go with his fictional alias, but we had to omit that part of the illusion, because he was using the sharp end of the arrow to self-mutilate. He would have attacked his ears instead, to spare him the mockery and ridicule he receives…but the thought of being deaf frightens him more than being laughed at."

They stepped over to the next iron cell. This man was holding firmly onto his bars, as he just stood there and stared aimlessly at his visitors. He looked as if he was trapped in a comatose state, where he was awake but not there. He also only had one eye, placed in the center of his face, just above the top of his nose bridge.

"This is Mister I."

"Yeah, I kind of gathered that," she said, as she swallowed her own saliva, captivated and exhilarated by seeing what she once thought was only fantasy lore.

"Mister I. was an accident, a mistake, a birth defect, if you will. His congenital disorder is characterized by the failure of the embryonic prosencephalon to properly divide the orbits of the eye into two cavities. The dismal thing is, it's not as rare as you would think, in human embryos."

Dawn looked at the cyclops' straggly, long blue hair, and inappropriately thought of Reuben. She fought to hold back the tears, as she realized that her departed beloved would have easily wound up in a nightmare like this, had he survived the mental asylum.

"Let's move on," the dwarf suggested, seeing the distraught on her face, as they came to the next dreary prison cell. "This is Windigo," he said, showing her the ten-foot freak who was painted to look like he was frozen. "Windigo is a cannibal, so when we let him out to perform, it's only in shackles and restraints. He's a malign creature. I never wanted him here, but that's just me."

"He's really a cannibal?" she asked, looking at the freakishly tall man who was sprawled out on the dirt floor, under heavy injected-sedation. She also noticed that Windigo was as endowed as he was towering.

"Oh yeah," Imp answered. "He's the real deal. Most of our freaks are."

They moved over to the next secured cage. This one made Dawn step back and gasp in disbelief. She rubbed her eyes, presuming that she must be delusional and that what she was witnessing couldn't possibly be authentic. Before her, was a gaunt albino, who had a six-inch, single horn extending from the middle of his forehead. He knelt in the middle of his cell, as if praying to the God that blatantly ignored him.

"Aah, yes," Imp said, sighing. "This one always gets plenty of attention and sympathy. Meet The Human Unicorn."

Dawn's eyes instantly leaked tears, as she gazed at this stunning man who looked like the epitome of fear and misery. He was dressed in a ragged loin cloth, which was shades of light gray and brownish-gray. Her broken heart ached for him, as she could sense that he was a man of purity and gentleness, and didn't belong there. He locked eye contact with her, and they both felt for each other's tormented existence. She managed to persuade him to pick himself up off the ground and come to meet her.

"What happened?" she asked Imp, as she reached out and touched the malnourished Unicorn man with her hand, softly petting the side of his melancholic face. He stood there on the other side of the bars, with his head hung in shame and his hope diminished.

"Yeah, um," Imp began, after clearing his throat, "he's afflicted with a rare condition known as *cornu cutaneum*, which causes conical protrusions to grow from the head and/or arms. In this case, it's obviously the head only, and he only has one growth. I know it looks like a horn made of coral, but it's actually made of keratin, the protein found in our hair and fingernails. Patients are usually advised to have them surgically removed, as they are tumors that can be malignant, but his can't be operated on. The risks are just too high, something to do with the growth being fused with part of his brain."

"That's it, I can't take anymore. Fuck this," she said, as Wolf followed her while she ran out of the enclosed sideshow attraction. Dawn was torn, because she wanted to free the Human Unicorn, and she could have easily done so, but she knew he would never survive in the wilderness of society. People were just too savage, and would have either beat him or dissected him, if he had encountered one of the countless sociopaths she knew all too well existed. Her tormented heart stung for the caged animals who were forced to perform for trade, never seeing benefits from their senseless sacrifice.

As she and Wolf reached the outside, she turned back to look at Imp, and he was gone. She once again pulled aside the draped entrance, to peek inside and see if she could spot the dwarf prankster, only to find a midget statue there in his place. The effigy looked like that of a Catholic saint. Had Dawn merely imagined Imp? Had he been nothing more than a figment of her deteriorating mental state? As she and Wolf trudged through the rest of the carnival, they breezed by and rubbed shoulders with those who had no outward deformities at all, but were equally as fascinating. There were those who blew and breathed fire, swallowed swords, juggled fireballs, and even levitated several inches off the ground. Customers had begun to swarm in, either to spectate or participate in the plethora of festivities. Dawn was approached by miscellaneous individuals who offered to share their dope.

"Hey, groovy chick, take a drag of this," one homeless vagrant said, while holding out a marijuana joint for her to accept.

"No thank you," she declined politely, "that's not really my bag, but I appreciate the offer."

"Dig it," he said in return, as he walked away and she rolled her eyes.

Vendors tried calling her over to their tables and booths, encouraging and begging her to take a gander at their handmade tye-dyed clothing and *Dead* beads. Dawn and Wolf were both feeling uncomfortable and overcrowded, as there were too many people around. As they made their way towards the exit, Wolf veered off to sniff out a psychedelic circus tent, that was set up alongside a large oak tree that seemed out of place. He was compelled to it, as if it had been embroidered with a scarlet letter. Dawn, out of sheer curiosity, decided to investigate why her beastly friend had deviated from their mutual decision to leave. Wolf was what was known as a *fylgja*, which meant *female follower*. He was Dawn's spiritual double in many ways, and therefore she would be a fool not to give his instinct the benefit of the doubt. Dawn had never considered seeking the psychic wisdom of a sideshow fortune teller, but at this point, saw only payoff in giving it a shot. She needed to know her fate's plan, even though she was a bit of a skeptic when it came to the transcendental.

"Enlarge your tent, stretch wide your curtains, and do not hold back. Lengthen your cords and strengthen your stakes," Dawn quoted Isaiah 54:2, while she held the tent's fabric in her grasp and hung her head against the exterior, pondering whether or not to enter.

"You know your Bible," a shrouded voice acknowledges, impressed with Dawn's ability to retain such literary detail on something that most Americans ignore, detest, or misrepresent.

"Well, it's kind of hard not to, being a preacher's daughter," she says back, smiling both briefly and nervously.

Just as Dawn was about to step inside the clairvoyant's domain for an insightful tarot reading, an engulfing chill came over her, like a raging and gelid wave, compelling her to continue her egress. She grabbed Wolf gently by the back of the neck, and guided him out to the parking area, choosing against the psychic visit. She walked in a trance-like state, as if being led by an invisible force and answering an unheard call. She and Wolf soon found themselves approaching the back of a blue 1975 *Dodge Ram* Van 150. The van had a small window on each side, near the back, that was in the shape of a psychedelic flower.

The rear doors were wide open, and inside perched an older but equally stunning woman. Her beauty was radiant, as she was basically the Caucasian counterpart of Dawn. She had large cat-like aquamarine eyes, and flowing pink hair that was fashionably feathered. She modeled white *Dittos* Saddleback jeans, which were skin-tight in all the right places. She wore fringed cowboy boots that matched Dawn's jacket, which had her pant-sleeves tucked in. She donned a purple leather vest, with nothing on underneath. Dawn immediately noticed her 34D cleavage, which revealed just about everything but her nipples. She also descried the woman's punk tattoo of barbed wire, which wrapped around the upper part of her left arm. Dawn, as if hypnotized against her will, stared into the stranger's maya-blue pupils. While they made eye contact and visually took each other in, Dawn intuitively felt as if this mysterious enchantress was somehow a kindred spirit.

"You want to help me put my puzzle together?" she asked the spellbound Dawn, while purposely enticing her into her van, so she could offer her own twisted version of Pandora's box.

Before Dawn could fully process what was happening, she and Wolf had both accepted the tempting nymph's invitation, still not knowing so much as her name. There were no back seats in the van, or if there had been, they had been removed. She had evidently remodeled the van to be a recreational vehicle. Dawn helped her fill and connect the missing pieces of the puzzle that the woman had already started, as the foxy stranger finally introduced herself.

"My name is Cheri," she said, pronouncing it like the sweet-tart fruit, "Cheri Celeste." As she spoke to Dawn, she rudely smacked her lips together while chewing *Bubblicious* gum with her mouth open.

Cheri's fashion sense fell somewhere between Joan Jett and a hotter version of Tammy Wynette, while her hair looked more like Farrah Fawcett's. The two newfound inamoratas glued the jigsaw pieces to the slab of pegboard, as they meticulously fit each of them in their proper place.

Dawn found herself hopelessly fascinated with Cheri's aerodynamic features, hourglass figure, and her pastel pink hair that rested over her shoulders and reminded her of her departed mother's hairstyle. Cheri's eye color nearly mirrored her own, which made Dawn feel an optical sisterhood with her, and made it that much more difficult to turn away from this beguiling creature. As they completed the jigsaw puzzle, Dawn and Wolf were mutually awestruck, when they saw that the final depiction was of Dawn and Cheri in an erotic and compromising embrace.

Cheri lasciviously lusted after the young Cherokee, even though she looked a bit mangy. She could recognize the mad dog in Dawn, but couldn't quite identify the werewolf. She had every confidence that she could tame the wild beast, while using Dawn's strength to suit her own selfish needs. Most would have been spooked by the mystical sexpot, but Dawn found her to be aberrantly attractive despite her sheer dominance and irresistible charisma. She was also mesmerized by the shiny rings on Cheri's fingers, which monopolized her left hand. Each knuckle was ornamented with a jewel; a moonstone, to awaken passion and tenderness in her chosen lover; a bloodstone with the likeness of a bat on the face, to give her power over demons and help her cause thunder and tempest; cat's eye, a stone that is greenish-yellow with a shot of blue, worn to test fidelity in a partner and make the wearer pellucid in battle; a howlite, to help relieve stress, pain and rage; and a black onyx, to symbolize her unhealthy obsession with, and detrimental fear of, mortality and death.

The ravenous 33-year-old gestured to her prospective prey with nothing more than a come-hither glance, and Dawn complied obediently by promptly disrobing. Dawn was consciously aware of what was taking place, but had no control over her own actions and responses. She briefly and tepidly struggled to defy, as she was somewhat skittish about opening herself up to Cheri, but soon found herself powerless. Cheri was easy on the eyes, which didn't help Dawn regain some sense of individuality. Dawn, being damaged and disturbed herself, as she gradually slipped deeper into madness, took a liking to this older woman's magnetism. Cheri removed her boots and tossed them aside, coming recklessly close to striking Wolf, who was laying down in the corner of the van with his paws covering his eyes. The rear doors were now shut and locked, and the heavily tinted windows only added to their discretion and privacy. Cheri's boots smelled of roses and had floral designs embroidered on the outside.

Dawn began having second thoughts about climbing into Cheri's mobile dominion. She resorts to using humor, as a preventive mechanism to keep Cheri in the dark about her uncertainty and instability, but her self-preservation efforts fall short. Seeing that Dawn was timid and tense about being there, Cheri decided to help ease her mental anguish through body massage. Before Dawn could absorb what was happening, Cheri had her laying on her stomach and was already bestriding her. They were both buck naked and Dawn could feel Cheri's soft-but-firm ass resting on her own youthful booty. Cheri treated and lubricated Dawn's lower back with scented oil, while licking her smooth skin, as she kneaded her shoulder and back muscles. As she worked around Dawn's spinal mane, and tended to her aching soreness, she found herself aroused by her feminine yet ferocious body. After an incessant thirty-minute period of Cheri rubbing little stars into the small of Dawn's back, she couldn't take it anymore. She made Dawn quiver, as she massaged the inked wolf paw emblem on her lower back, which may as well have been a target. The unshakable thirst she felt for Dawn had overcome her, and she needed to divide and devour. Before Dawn could fully process the events taking place in that blue *Dodge* van, Cheri was answering the call of the wild and gently nibbling on Dawn's ear, while firmly holding her face in her capable hands. Cheri's seduction of Dawn happens hastily, as if the very constellations had authored their serendipity. It's lust at first sight for both of them, and Dawn finds it impossible to keep herself in check as Cheri robs her of her control. As they tenderly and aggressively explore each other's tonsils, while they exchange a warm embrace, Cheri feels Dawn's hot tears on her trembling cheek.

"What's wrong?" Cheri asked. "Am I hurting you?"

Dawn didn't answer, but Cheri could feel her self-deprecating thoughts. She couldn't tell why exactly, but she was able to sense that Dawn felt unworthy of happiness or pleasure. Dawn tried to pull away a time or two, but Cheri wouldn't allow it. She was going to have her way with Dawn, whether she consented or not. Dawn, of course, could have wiped Cheri from existence, but something drew her to the pink-haired half-breed that she couldn't elucidate. As the odd couple got more cozy in the back of the van, they further surrendered to their creature comforts. Cheri took a momentary break from bewitching Dawn, to turn on her stereo, which had just begun to play the Donny Osmond cover of, *Puppy Love*. Cheri put Dawn's hand down the front of her pants, so the sexy American Indian could feel her Brazilian-styled pussy that groomed her bikini area. This was uncommon, as most women didn't bother to trim their pubic region, much less shave or wax it. The irony here was that Dawn was the one much younger in age, while Cheri was the one who felt like a baby.

Coercing her into rolling over on her back, Cheri wasted no time in laying atop her, seizing her by the face with both hands, and French kissing her with extreme intensity and passion. Dawn felt Cheri's toasty tongue in her moist mouth, and was spellbound by her fruity kiss. Even though Cheri's hair was the color of grapefruit, her pliable tongue tasted of raspberry flavor. Dawn tried to withstand at first, but realized that she was only battling to repudiate her reciprocated thirst, based on the way she was raised. She had tried to push Cheri away, but with minimal effort, as that wasn't really what she wanted. Once Cheri felt she had Dawn under her spell, her grip on the sides of her head softened and became clement. Dawn turned her face to try and escape her canoodling, but that didn't last long, as she soon returned Cheri's persistent affections. Cheri fondled and kneaded Dawn's scalp, as they continued swapping saliva.

Dawn made one final and feigned attempt to resist Cheri's assertive craving, by pushing on her shapely breasts. As the Cherokee jezebel cupped Cheri's symmetrical boobs in her hands, she felt an erect third nipple, found directly underneath her left one. Though this would have concerned and repelled most, it only further stimulated Dawn's libido. Cheri just responded by taking Dawn's wrists into her grip and holding them down on either side of her. She could tell that Dawn wanted her, and was only putting up a fight to try and convince herself that she wasn't bisexual. Cheri took a breather from tickling Dawn's tonsils with her tongue, and stared into Dawn's eyes as they had locked with her own. Cheri could see into her soul, as Dawn became more mesmerized by her hypnotic mojo.

Cheri pushed herself up with her arms that had been revitalized by the invigorating energy that Dawn organically exuded. Dawn noticed that Cheri had dead eyes, meaning they had no light reflecting off them, almost as if they had been painted on by a Michelangelo copycat. Was this older woman an impostor, merely posing as a human? Was she a zombie? Dawn didn't know, and what was most unsettling was that she didn't care. Besides, who was she to judge?

"You're intoxicating," Cheri complimented her with genuine and endearing sentiment.

Dawn felt weak, drained, and exhausted. Cheri, on the other hand, felt anything but lethargic. Dawn had reluctantly and unknowingly fed her, and Cheri wanted more. She was automatically addicted to Dawn, and found her to be a better high than any chemical or herbal substance that she had ever indulged in or experimented with.

As Dawn laid there limp and flat on her back, Cheri noticed hair that was stuck to her hands. She brought it up to her face to better examine it and deciphered that it was animal hair. She turned her head and looked at Wolf, who was still cowering in the corner, wisely staying out of their way. Cheri could tell that the hair wasn't from Wolf, as it was brown and not white. It was this pivotal moment when Cheri identified that Dawn was much more than she appeared to be on the surface. She still didn't know for certain what Dawn's secret was, but she knew beyond the shadow of a doubt that she was hiding something pretty sensational and spectacular.

"Wow," she said, unaware that she was speaking out loud, "you're one sick puppy, aren't yah?"

Dawn turns her face to the left and pouts her lips, as if to express that her fragile feelings had been wounded. Cheri could tell that Dawn was thinking that she had lost interest in her and didn't like her anymore. Cheri tranquilly and solicitously took hold of her by the chin and turned her head, so that she had to face her. Dawn still looked away, embarrassed and ashamed that her werewolf identity had turned Cheri off.

"Look at me, bitch," Cheri commanded, aggressively but affectionately. Dawn finally met her glance, with sad, puppy dog eyes. "This only makes me want you more, baby."

As far as Cheri was concerned, she had hit the jackpot. Dawn's supernatural power would only enhance and extend her usefulness for Cheri. Though they were stretched out in the back of the van, Cheri used telekinesis to turn the key, which she had left in the ignition. She then used her mind to operate her compact cassette player, and pushed in the *Cliff Richard* tape that was in there. The 1976 song, *Devil Woman*, began playing, which was aimed as a mood-setter, but instead only underlined the hidden nature of the lap of treachery that Dawn had crawled into.

Cheri threw her arms and head back, and for a fleeting moment, reminded the ruined Cherokee of the resurrected Son of God whom she had grown to feel prodigiously forsaken by. Cheri just enjoyed the pulsating power that she absorbed and embezzled from Dawn, who had no indicator to warn her of Cheri's cruel guise. Though she had nothing at her disposal to view her own reflection, Cheri could feel her eyes turn a vibrant and lucid shade of emerald green. Her eyes had the tendency to go jade at the point of climax.

When Cheri leaned forward to continue ravaging her victim, she took a firm hold of Dawn's breasts, and began to violently suck and gnaw on them. She nibbled on the nipples and around the areola, as if having to consciously fight not to take it too far and bite them off. Dawn tasted that good to her, and could savor and relish her essence through all of her senses. She suckled and chewed on her nipples for a few more minutes, as if nursing two bottle teats. Cheri kissed every inch of her body until she made her way down to her pubic region. Dawn, being as hairy as she was, didn't dissuade Cheri from being interested, but she did find it to be outside of her comfort zone. Cheri was used to dining on pussies that were much like her own, because she would either demand they were smooth or she would shave it herself. Spreading the bushy hair to the side, Cheri went to town on eating Dawn out, burying her face and tongue into her gash, as if she would never again have the opportunity to enrapture her exemplary cunt. Dawn, as tired as she was, was still able to feel the blissful delight and was in complete hedonistic heaven.

After her jaw turned sore from going south on her for too long, Cheri rolled her over and put her face in Dawn's first-rate ass. She spread her delectable cheeks, so she could continue munching on the scrumptious she-wolf from behind. Dawn quivered with spasms, meditating on the diabetic sensation Cheri was delivering, not wishing to miss a moment or a touch. The infernal Cheri licked her raw, paying specific attention to Dawn's happy button.

"Oh yeah, lemme smoke that crack," Cheri said, as her voice boomed and blended with heavy panting and breathing.

Dawn snatched one of the two pillows and chomped down on it, as Cheri enthusiastically probed her hygienic backdoor with her index and middle fingers. She brazenly spread Dawn's anatomical wonderland with her other hand, while spelling the alphabet on her clit with her overly-eager tongue that was forked at the tip.

"Do you like the crack of Dawn?" she asked the authoritative pink-haired floozy, in a little girl voice, as she feels the juices build up inside of her, which were begging for an eruptive release.

After Dawn has an explosive orgasm in her mouth, Cheri gets up and positions herself over Dawn's head, not bothering to brush the vaginal secretions from her soused lips and glazed chin.

"Get under me, bitch," Cheri ordered, wanting Dawn to sniff her sweaty ass, and using the word *bitch* as a term of endearment and a method of degradation.

As Cheri straddles her knees over Dawn's head, she rests her soggy and throbbing vagina directly over Dawn's mouth and sits comfortably on her face. As Dawn began to reciprocate the oral favor, Cheri reaches down and tugs on Dawn's bone choker, which she saw as more of a dog collar. She was at least perceptive and sensitive enough to not jerk it too hard, as she could sense that it had sentimental value and spiritual meaning for Dawn. Though she was careful not to break or bogart it, she couldn't help but dig the necklace, as it not only fit Dawn's aura, but also perfectly suited Cheri's kinky facade.

Her inked tribal armband gave the misleading illusion that Cheri had a tough exterior, but Dawn saw something in her that Cheri couldn't see in herself. Dawn basked in the presence and ambiance of her occultic lover, completely consumed and smitten by the sexual paradise that seemed to be immediate and undeniable. Dawn tasted something tangy and terrible, funny and foul. Cheri had started her period, while Dawn was feasting on her womanhood. Dawn tried to close her jaw and stop lapping her cycle juices, but Cheri took hold of her head and pulled it up against her saturated crotch, signaling an unspoken expectation for her to continue. Dawn complied, as she obediently reopened her lips and resumed tantalizing her clitoris orally, while the menstrual blood filled her waiting yet reluctant mouth.

"Oh yeah," Cheri sighed in optimal glee, as she fed Dawn her monthly stream, "part that red sea. Drink from that cherry creek!"

Cheri leaned her head back again and cackled, holding and guiding the back of Dawn's skull. She pulled on Dawn's hair, while she bit her lower lip, captivated by the satisfying gratification that she never wanted to end. Cheri thrived on her hypnotic suggestion over Dawn and reveled in the ultimate pleasure she was supplying her. Though Dawn wasn't exactly enthusiastic about snacking on Cheri during her monthly cycle, the period blood actually wasn't as revolting as what she had been forced to do with Nurse Carl in the supplies closet. Dining on Cheri's menses had an even more unexpected effect, as if Dawn had been slipped some LSD and it was finally kicking in. She began to see Cheri as a demon, with everything from the horns to the cloven feet. The experience was more surreal than sensual, yet it still served as a mind-blowing fantasy. Dawn fingered herself with one hand while she lapped up Cheri's discharge, and used her other hand to spread the pussy lips of her naughty, pink-haired minx.

After about ninety minutes of uninhibited and unconventional lovemaking, Dawn and her lightning dominatrix reached simultaneous and exhilarating culmination, thereby marking the origin of their dysfunctional courtship. Dawn found herself snuggling with Cheri, as if this instant romance had been predestined and undeniable. The adorable Indian squaw had fallen asleep in Cheri's arms, with her pretty head resting on her naked and ample bosom. The blue-eyed enchantress held Dawn tight and close, as Wolf curled up in the corner of the van, no longer apprehensive around Cheri, but still sagacious enough to stay out of her way.

Dawn ended up spending the night, sleeping with the rosy hybrid. She momentarily woke from her slumber, finding herself being spooned by Cheri. She hadn't anticipated bonding with anyone again, but there was something inebriating and irresistible about Cheri that she couldn't deny or refuse. Dawn was tired of being a desolate pariah, and felt like she was dying inside without that unconditional love she so craved and hadn't felt since Reuben. It was nice to be held again, and made to feel special and wanted. She accepted that her fate was dismal and pessimistic, but what frightened her was the thought of spending eternity alone. She was grateful for Wolf and cherished their genuine kinship, but Dawn needed someone her own kind to surrender the reigns to again. She desperately needed someone to tend to her sexual needs again, who would need her rather than use her. She needed someone like Reuben, as hard as that was to imagine existed. She was understandably uncertain about her split decision to shack up with Cheri, but her nomadic van was a more appealing alternative to sleeping in alleyways with the homeless and turning tricks for money.

Dawn woke up the next morning, wearing Cheri's purple vest and nothing else. Not unlike her boots, Cheri's leather vest had the elaborate design of a rose bush embroidered on the back. Cheri made a perfect match for her, as neither one was shallow enough to bother with cosmetics. Cheri kept a *nude lip*, showing a little bit of gloss to give some shine, but no extra or added color. They both had the ability to appreciate natural beauty, as well as value what was on the inside. With just a look, they told each other how gorgeous they saw one another, even with their hair a mess and their breath not the freshest. Dawn's breasts were sore and tender, from the bruised hickeys that Cheri had proudly left her with. There were clumps of hair laying on and around her body, but not the wolf hair that would periodically shed from her scalp. This time, the pubic hair was coming off, not by falling out, but by having been charred. The stunning, and evidently searing, Cheri had singed Dawn's pelvic region...just by laying on top of her. Though her hairs had made a mess in Cheri's van, Dawn was pleased to see the piles and patches they had left behind. For the first time in God knows how long, Dawn could see her own vagina without having to adjust and struggle. Her armpit hair had completely withered away and burned off, without a hint of flame. Dawn's delightful but dubious connection with Cheri wasn't utopian, but it was what she needed nonetheless. Cheri somehow filled the hole that Reuben had inadvertently left through his untimely and traumatic death.

The pink-haired alpha was reading an issue of *Teen Beat* magazine, reading about her favorite actress, Kristy McNichol, whom she seemed to be somewhat obsessed over. She was topless still, but had slid on a pair of corduroy shorts. Dawn found her body scorched, with somewhere between second and third-degree burns, which seemed to be primarily distributed on her breasts and ass. The smoldering burns were conveniently and clearly in the shape of hands, which was appropriate considering where they were and who made them. Though the burns appeared to be caused by a blazing fire, there had been no inferno. Cheri's secret identity had been as disguised as Dawn's inner beast. Much like a naive donor to an energy vampire, Dawn found herself not only helpless to Cheri's will, but was unable to resist wanting more, even though her hankering for Cheri was literally causing her harm. Their connection was covetous and prolific, and Dawn desperately needed that again. Most girls, Dawn's age, would have turned and run the other direction after finding their body sizzled. Though Dawn couldn't express or explain it, this was one flame that she was more than willing to be burned by. Besides, at least Dawn was losing some of her body hair, which for once, wasn't automatically growing back. She felt a primal fear when it came to Cheri, but she also felt queerly at home with her.

Dawn gasped for breath, gripping her chest and pulling it outward, as if to somehow compensate for the restricted tightness. She would have screamed in torment, but Cheri's sadistic scheme had left her in a silent hush. Cheri played with herself, stroking and fondling her tender and swollen clit, trying to prolong the throbbing sensation that Dawn had gifted her. During their fetish-themed encounter, Dawn had misinterpreted it as something more, as Cheri had provisionally made her forget about her mission of vindicating her impaled Reuben. Not only had Dawn's obliterated heart resumed its aching, but she found herself engulfed in a dark shadow that wasn't just her own. As Dawn watched Cheri use her own hand to entertain herself, down the front of her pink shorts, she hoped that she wouldn't trample her already damaged heart. Dawn suddenly felt like she had fallen into a loony bin all over again, and decided to try and escape from the very source of her recent joy. Using what little strength she had left, Dawn jumped out of her mobile home, and stumbled and limped to get away from Cheri.

After watching Dawn collapse from being drained of her life force, Cheri comes to her aid, scoops her up in her arms, and chivalrously carries her back to her van. The floor of the van was lined and insulated with shag carpeting. Cheri sings her to sleep, like an attentive mother, while *rearing* her like a dirty old man. She gently, but deeply, probes Dawn's tight anus with her middle finger and then sticks it in the Cherokee's hot mouth, forcing her to suck it.

"You like that lollipop, baby?" Cheri asked her, as Dawn obeyed while trying to stay alert and awake. "Let's try a different flavor," she said grinning. "You're gonna love this one." Cheri reached down and pried her own butthole wide open. As she abusively stretched her own anus, she pushed out her prolapse. Squatting over Dawn's face, she made Dawn suck on it, as if she were stranded in the blazing desert and Cheri's protruded asshole was a water-carrying cactus.

Dawn's hateful indignation flashed before her eyes, as she meditated on Nurse Carl and her resentment towards God. She dwelled on her fear and her bitterness, her insatiable appetite for retribution, and the personalized aftermath from waking up to the reality that there is no justice. As she stewed in this complicated mess of names, places, institutions, events, and incidences, she felt Cheri's body heat in their passionate clutch. If either woman had had an ice cube to shove up her cooch, it wouldn't take any time at all to melt. Emotions exploded in Dawn like a backdraft, as Cheri opened the doors to new horizons. Her guilt, shame, and inadequacies were temporarily, but effectively, swept over by this intimately compulsive behavior that was sourcing from Cheri's domineering control. Cheri's power was electrifying and infectious, as her waves of carnality were addicting...yet somehow questionable. Though Dawn couldn't decide whether or not she deemed Cheri to be trustworthy, all of her defects, attitudes, and losses were briefly misplaced, while Cheri introduced her to an entirely new world of pleasure and pain.

Later that night, Cheri drives to a cemetery and lays out a large wool blanket. She leaves the key partially turned in the ignition, when they leave the van, to fill their night with soft tunes. Don McLean's, *Vincent*, plays over the radio, as they spread out amongst the assortment of graves. Wolf gives them privacy, as he ventures off to explore the various tombstones. Dawn and Cheri relax and snuggle together under the silvery moonlight, engaging in heavy petting as they spoon and cradle each other. It's particularly windy that night, but Dawn and Cheri both remain unbothered by the obnoxiously cold weather, as their body temperatures are both supernaturally sheathed. Dawn couldn't tell if what she was seeing was real, or if her vision was playing tricks on her, but she saw something in the night sky that was impossible. She blinked forcefully and repeatedly, hoping that it would bring her back to reality, but what she was seeing was real. There were three moons in the sky, two crescents with their backs to the full moon in the center.

"Isn't the shiny moon dazzling?" Cheri asked her. "The sharp arc of a new moon can pierce the thickest armor of cynicism with a sense of promise. The radiant full moon is an ancient power for making magic, and a night without a moon will remind you of the infinite abyss, where dreams, death, mystery, magic, and rebirth all dwell," Cheri said, as her eyes rolled to the back of her head, and she looked to be hypnotized by someone else's thoughts and controlled by words that were not her own. She snapped out of her trance, just in time to hear Dawn share a secret about her father.

"Daddy loved me too much," Dawn confided out of the blue, "or didn't love me enough."

Cheri chose to remain silent and unresponsive, even though she could secretly relate. Her own father was extremely violent and abusive, but he was also a demon. Cheri's father had been invoked by a Satanic breeder to help her murder her mother and stepfather with a meat cleaver. This ancient ceremony involved Cheri's mother sitting in a 9-foot pentacle, with kindled candles on each of the five points, an eerie incantation, and application of magical ointment to her nude body, which she then cloaked with a sheepskin. The conjured incubus then penetrated and impregnated the impudent 16-year-old who summoned him, before she's eventually caught and prosecuted to life imprisonment. Cheri was born in the prison and taken from her mother at birth, placed into foster care. She never knew her mother and only saw her father during surreal nightmares or through lucid dreaming.

She caresses Dawn, as they hold each other with a sense of urgency and codependency. Just then, Cheri spots a hairy wolf spider on their blanket and sees it crawling towards Dawn. Though the large spider wasn't poisonous, it was frightening in size and appearance. Suddenly, Cheri felt concerned for and even protective towards Dawn, which had crept up on her unexpectedly. Not wanting her new playmate terrified, Cheri quickly snatched the spider up, while Dawn gently sucked on her ample breasts as if Cheri's nipples were pacifiers. The raspberry dominatrix brought her hand up to her mouth, as if pretending to politely cover a yawn, and popped the scary spider in between her lips. Cheri then gently, but effectively, crushed the beastly arthropod with her killing bite.

"Are you tired, mistress?" Dawn asked, taking a break from nibbling on her supple tits. Being distracted by Cheri's delectable body, she never saw the spider or heard the audible crunch.

"A little," Cheri answered, after quickly swallowing the thick and juicy arachnid.

At that moment, the newfound concubines simultaneously gazed up and were astonished to catch sight of stellar activity occurring in the stars. They watched, dumbfounded, as three bright lights made a triangular formation in the night sky. This was unexplainable, since no manmade aircraft or human technology could have achieved the scientific phenomenon that they had just bore witness to. As Cheri holds her lover tight and close, she feels a growing wetness underneath them. She soon becomes aware that Dawn, who is scared shitless, is urinating where they sit. The unidentified flying objects disappear as abruptly and mysteriously as they had materialized.

"It's okay, my darling," Cheri consoled her prized specimen, as Dawn trembles in her arms, "everything's gonna be alright." She was just as dazzled by the alien encounter as Dawn was, but was simply better at hiding her disconcerting alarm.

Cheri got up and walked to her van to get a spare blanket from the custom interior. Dawn concentrated on her bare ass, as she hated to see Cheri go, but loved to watch her leave. While she waited for her to come back, she did something even more batty, and rolled around in her puddle of piss. Cheri could identify the progression of lunacy and deterioration of sanity in Dawn's tired eyes, but there was something about her that was worth her trouble. Dawn's robust energy sufficiently restored and sustained Cheri's welfare and peace of mind. This, in turn, both affirmed and sealed her decision to use Dawn as her slave donor.

OCTOBER 22, 1978
CHERRY MOON

What had initially begun as a search for insight, regarding her fate, had instantly sprouted into a powerful and enigmatic connection that Dawn could have never foreseen. Something she couldn't explain had ignited between her and Cheri; something invigorating, esoteric, and unhindered. A current had flowed through the back doors of that groovy van, the moment they had locked eye contact, as if a synergy-filled electric charge had transcendentally linked them. This Fall was the time for ardor and fervor, and these two fillies were going to enjoy their season in the sun.

Their senses went wild, as the two mavericks shared raw primal energies that made their intimacy an exchange deeper than sex. They each felt as if they were dining on ambrosia, as they delighted in the elation of going down on one another. Their lovemaking could never compare to what she had felt with Reuben, but it came pretty close to being as magical. It was as if the mere smell and taste of each other had provided a biological aphrodisiac, which only further aroused and enhanced their cosmic passion.

Cheri, in her persuasive dominance, convinced Dawn to move in with her, and of course extended the invite to Wolf. Cheri lived in a modest two-bedroom apartment with an Irish female who was literally only there to sleep, and usually not even then. Since her flatmate was basically absent, and just good for splitting the bills, it couldn't have been a better situation for Dawn and Cheri to shack up and officially launch their exclusively unconventional relationship. The upper and lower kitchen cabinets were unfinished wood. The painted wall and laminate countertops were a pumpkin orange. The fiberglass chairs were a seafoam green. The kitchen table was round, and was a taffy shade of pink. There was a set of four *Vera Neumann* vinyl placemats that were designed with floral prints and patterns. The table was on one side of the dividing counter, while the wall oven and light switch were both on the other and surrounded by red brick.

The layout of the living room was pretty simple and basic. It was furnished with a bright yellow, button tufted sofa, with an astronomical symbol for the sun hanging on the wall behind it (which subliminally resembled a woman's nipple). There was a peacock wicker-rattan doll chair, accompanied by a wicker foot stool. Then, there was a new model *Sylvania* B&W 23" console with lighted dials, which was encased in a wooden unit that was fitted with a skinny drawer underneath. On top of the television set, sat a lava lamp that was intended to mesmerize female visitors, while Cheri sat with them on the corduroy couch and had their heads lay on her bare hope chest. Cheri reminisced about when she'd watch *Love American Style*, which was a comedy sketch show that temporarily helped her forget how lonely she really was.

Cheri's bedroom was decked out with multiple variations of the color purple, accompanied by wadded up bubblegum wrappers on the neglected hardwood floor. The wardrobe closet was exposed and had enough extra space for Dawn, especially since they didn't require many clothes. The stretch of carpet, underneath the bed, was Mid-Century Scandinavian rya shag rug, which was designed to imitate rose pedals. The beaded paneling was plywood with a pine pattern laminate, and the ceiling was fixed with popcorn texture. The dressers, nightstand, and door were all unstained and unpainted wood. The purple-themed bedspread was quilted with black satin sheets underneath. The queen-sized bed had a black headboard that was perfect for handcuffing wrists to. The curtains were illustrated with roses and thorns, as were the tacky *Instant Stained Glass* window decals in the four corners. There were a couple of arched wicker shelves, which each held a ceramic owl candle that burned incense that diffused either a vanilla or lilac fragrance. In between these two wall hangings was a framed poster of the famous Jim Morrison, *Open Arms*, pose.

It was no coincidence that there were no mirrors in the shared apartment. Cheri wouldn't allow it, as she couldn't stomach looking at her own reflection. On the surface, she presented the illusion that she had it all together, but Cheri was torn inside and battled inner demons that nobody knew about. Their romance was progressing as quickly and as fiery as it had immediately ignited. They wasted no effort, and lived each moment to its fullest, devoting as much time as they could to concentrating on their sexual exploits and experimentations. Though the apartment had a cramped laundry room, which was separated only by a bamboo-beaded curtain, they had little use for its' services, seeing as how Cheri encouraged Dawn to remain bottomless while they were home. Cheri took it upon herself to buy Dawn a few outfits for when they would be out and about in public, including a pair of stonewashed *Levi* Button Fly jeans, which Dawn went crazy over.

They didn't have access to a fireplace, but they didn't need one. No bonfire would come close to paralleling the sensual heat that naturally transpired between them. The beauty they beheld in each other's eyes was far more magical than any beach or sunset. They didn't need a sandy boardwalk or a stroll down the isle, to spark or sustain their romance. They had each other, and that was more than enough to distract them from the pain that tormented their souls.

***

They had just gotten back from a County Fair the day before, where Cheri watched Dawn frolic on a moon bounce and feast on a candy apple. It hadn't even occurred to Dawn, in her fun with the pink-haired parasite, that this was the first time she had been able to stomach regular food and keep it down. Cheri watched the childish object of her lustful desire, while Dawn cradled the plush wolf that she had won for her. The stuffed animal even had pink fur that matched Cheri's hair color, making the gift even more special. Cheri, being as shamelessly bold as she was, didn't wait for an invitation to clean Dawn's mouth with her forked tongue. As they left the public event and made their way back to the van, a black cat came out of nowhere and ran directly in front of the two affectionate lesbians. Cheri and Dawn had both been walking side by side, with their hand resting on each other's ass. After seeing the dark feline practically scurry over their feet, Dawn stopped to appreciate the little guy.

"Aww," she said, while kneeling down and outstretching her hand to try and entice the cat to trust her, so she could stroke its head and back. "Pretty kitty."

As soon as the black cat heard Dawn's soothing voice, he stopped and turned around. Looking up at his friendly admirer, he began to cautiously walk towards them.

"You like pussy, don't you, baby?" Cheri asked, grinning wickedly and already knowing her answer. "I'm pretty sure you prefer pink to black, though."

After the cat heard Cheri's melodic but menacing voice, the kitty stopped in his tracks, sensing the disguised danger that escorted Dawn. Taking one last look at the well-meaning American Indian, as if to offer an unspoken apology, he took off. Dawn looked up at Cheri, saddened and disappointed.

"I've always been more of a dog person anyway," Cheri said, smiling, in attempt to cheer her up. Dawn blushes, while she humbly bows her head, as Cheri pets and scratches it. "And I have a humdinger right here," Cheri added, basically calling her lover a dog, but using the word as a term of endearment.

They continued their date into the evening hours, at a roller disco, where they equally and mutually acted like giddy schoolgirls. They also behaved as if they were in love, as they skated side by side to ABBA's song, *Take A Chance On Me*, while holding hands. Cheri noticed a creepy older man ogling Dawn, from one of the cafe tables, while pretending to be looking through a kaleidoscope that he had either purchased there or brought from home. As they got closer to passing by where he sat, Cheri's eyes not only turned green again, but they became reptilian. The dirty old man suddenly got a feeling, which wasn't stemming from his hand that was down the front of his pants. He put the tin cylinder down, and as he did, he realized that his eyes were still seeing the loose and glassy colored objects that he had seen in the psychedelic chamber. He blinked heavily and repeatedly, trying to shake this bad trip, but each time he reopened his eyes, his eyesight was still trapped in that toy. Putting his palms up to cover his cursed eyes, he screamed in frantic terror, causing the wait staff to rush to his distressed aid. In his blinded frenzy, he bumped the table and spilled his can of *Jolly Good* grape soda on his crotch. Cheri and Dawn continued skating, remaining calm and unaffected by the vengeful chaos that the hellish hybrid's jealousy had inspired.

Many of the young women at that rink wore satin jogging shorts, which may as well have been stripper underwear. Nearly everyone wore striped socks that came to their knees or pulled above. A few of the guys had fedora hats and suspenders. Members of both genders modeled sweat bands on their heads and wrists. Some wore knee protection, but many went without pads. Most of the people had on flashy shirts, which were either overly shiny or a little too revealing. The crowd got thicker, as more took the floor to shake their booty and boogie to the funky music. Much like how it got to be at the carnival, Dawn eventually felt claustrophobic. She realized that she had spent the entire day without Wolf, who had been left alone at Cheri's apartment. It was the first time he and Dawn had been apart since they first hooked up. Knowing that she hadn't suffered any separation anxiety, scared her, because it reaffirmed her undeniable and unbreakable bond with Cheri. Andy Gibb's, *Shadow Dancing*, played while the two hotties made one final loop around the rink.

As Cheri returned the skates to the rental counter, Dawn was moved and impressed with how much effort she was putting into their affair. Cheri was investing a lot of time, funds, and thought into Dawn, and she had already gotten into her pants…many times. This fact didn't escape Dawn, but rather only made her appreciate Cheri more. They shared a heavy vibe between them that was irresistible and insatiable, and Dawn wasn't complaining. She slid off the short white socks that Cheri had given her to wear under the skates, and put her groovy, *Candie's* platform sandals back on. Even though Cheri was secretly using her, she was also genuinely nurturing and sincerely considerate towards young Dawn. They soon returned home, where they immediately got barefoot and frisky.

The next few days were devoted to perpetual and wooing engagement, while time flew by like it was nothing. They trespassed on a private orchard, to pick stolen apples, while Wolf ate more than they collected in the wicker basket. They had hit the produce jackpot, as this particular and entrepreneurial grower was obsessed with and addicted to not just apples, but many kinds and versions of apples. This was an eclectic and bountiful orchard, which offered a variety of apples, including *Granny Smith, Honeycrisp, Liberty,* and *Snapdragon.* Cheri took further advantage of the owners being away, by hot-wiring their pickup, so that Dawn and Wolf could relax in the bed and sit on the tailgate, while experiencing a hayride. When the sun descended and nightfall came, they made love on a flowerbed of purple *False Dragonhead.* Like usual, they exhausted one another in their steamy passion, and Dawn continued to be systematically drained of her strength and energy. Dawn's bushy armpit hair hadn't returned, as if it had never existed, and Dawn wasn't complaining. Even though she could discern that there was something amiss, she was distracted by the benefits and perks of being Cheri's love, and chose not to analyze the agony and torment that came with it.

"This feels right," Dawn says out loud in a soft whisper, while Cheri held her tenderly from behind, as they stood together and watched Wolf romp and play as if he were their surrogate child.

They were confident enough in their ability to protect themselves and each other, that it didn't concern them regarding when the owners would pull up onto the property. Cheri pushed Dawn on a tire swing that hung from a big tree on the privately owned land. For all they knew, the homeowners could have been out of town or currently on their way back. Whatever the case was, they weren't worried or stressed about the risk. All they cared about was the moment they were in, and doing what they could to make it last as long as possible. Dawn felt happy with Cheri, but when faced away from her or out of her peripheral sight, she snuck in a tear or two for her dead son and for Reuben's loving memory. The two lipstick lesbians slow danced under the moon, while wishing in unspoken prayer that their carefree bliss would never have to end, even though they both knew that it wouldn't last forever. As far as Cheri was concerned, Dawn was condemned to indefinite servitude, and her genuine fondness for the tribal princess wasn't going to alter that.

OCTOBER 31, 1978
SAMHAIN
BLOOD MOON

The Modern-American Christian community is all too often erroneous and ignorant about their misconceived and misguided perception of reality. That's not at all meant to be an insult towards God, as the good Lord is commonly either victimized, distorted, or underestimated by these self-proclaimed Christians who mock anything and everything they don't understand. If it's not recorded in black and white, they convince themselves that it can't be true, as if God is incapable of being mysterious. These pseudo-Christians view Freemasons to be inherently evil and Halloween to be the most diabolical of Satanic holidays, which are quite sadly only two of the many examples of this unfortunate truth. Christians often get caught up in their own personal interpretations and countless translations of what they wish to believe God is or what his Gospel says, with no regard to what Jesus actually represents or what Scripture is really for.

It was that time of year again, where authentic ghouls and goblins caused havoc among the little children, while they begged for candy and punished those who neglected or denied their demands. This was what Christians chose to believe anyway, while they were preoccupied doing their own horrific deeds behind closed doors and manipulating others into believing twisted versions of the Gospel, to suit their own self-serving agendas. Despite popular belief, *All Hallow's Eve* was not defined by its sensational mythology or ridiculous propaganda. In fact, it was the established Christian dates that were often the replacements for ancient pagan holidays... that were reserved for the same calendar days...which were held in high esteem or considered to be special or sacred.

This isn't to allege that atrocities didn't happen on Halloween, but they were often the deeds and consequences of the unusual suspects, who thrived on jumping on the Satanic bandwagon and feeding the irrational hysteria. Children were sometimes sexually abused and even abducted on this holiday, or injured and murdered by contaminated or sabotaged candy. This, however, was almost always the devious actions of unfit and demented parents, or contributed by corrupt factories and wicked corporations. The Christian church used these horrific and newsworthy stories to further promote their propaganda, which typically had nothing to do with anything that had occurred.

Cheri was much like Reuben, in the sense that she thoroughly enjoyed playing the grown-up role to the significantly younger, yet legally-aged, Dawn. To celebrate the playful occasion, Cheri dug out an old costume from a locked trunk, which she hadn't laid eyes or hands on in a dozen years. It wasn't a mask so much as it was headgear. The piece was made of hard latex, and fit over the top of her head. It was designed to look like the musical god, *Pan*, with goat horns and pointed, elongated ears. The costume came with footwear that were made to look like cloven hooves. Cheri even had a working flute to go with the seasonal ensemble, which she lent to Dawn as well.

Reuben's brutal murder had paralyzed Dawn, for what seemed to have already been an eternity without him. The trauma of his loss had led her to fall apart, and break down bit by bit. Wolf and Cheri had slowly begun to change that, giving her reason to go on and hope that things might be okay, if not get better. Dawn felt like she had found her family…her pack…and they were literally saving her from self-destruction. Being with Cheri distracted her from killing at all, as the raspberry queen of lust appeared to have domesticated the wild and unruly Cherokee. Then, there was Wolf, who was like her child…well, her other child…the one who lived. The mettlesome girl found cathartic release in murder, but knew it was only a matter of time before she was caught, trapped, and made extinct. She was happy to have reasons not to indulge in her unabating and ceaseless reparation. Wolf certainly wasn't complaining, as he didn't miss Linda's deterring phantom, who would always make his heart race and his hair frizz out.

Cheri chaperoned Dawn to some of the nearby neighborhoods, walking with and encouraging her to go to each house with the small children. Dawn was met with some very surprised greetings, but considering that most of the people who answered the doors were men, they gleefully tolerated and humored her. She was entirely too old to be trick or treating, but she was also ravishing and impossible to not envy with desire. Dawn looked mouthwatering, and charmed all the divorced husbands, neglected and betrayed boyfriends, and alienated and abandoned fathers, even while having her beautiful face covered with painted latex. As they made their way from house to house, Dawn played the flute and as the night progressed, actually built a following of children marching behind her. She led the little people, like sheep, for a term…at least until their parents called them back or chased them down and whisked them away from the goat-headed stranger. Up ahead, Dawn sees a little girl being bullied, while one of her tormenters is photographing the violence with her mother's *Kodak pocket Istamatic c*amera. She instinctively runs up to the young victim, while the entourage of mean girls cowardly scatter like startled chickens.

"Are you okay, honey?" she asks, as she helps the shaken girl off the ground. "What's your name, sweetheart?" Dawn inquired, wondering where her parents were, who had appeared to have let their daughter participate in the sugar-begging without any escort or supervision.

"Persephone Morgan," the distressed child answered.

"Who were those girls? Did they hurt you?" Dawn asked, genuinely concerned.

"They tripped and pushed me. They said they were going to beat me up, which they would have if you hadn't come," she answered, expressing her profound gratitude.

Persephone's impassioned smile quickly turned to a frightened startle, as she looked up and made eye contact with Dawn. Looking into her magical eyes, the little girl could see that Dawn wasn't the average Jane. She couldn't tell that Dawn was a werewolf, but she could see that the friendly stranger had a fierce beast inside of her, which significantly scared Persephone. Dawn's eyes were enchanting as ever, but had grown to be equally as menacing.

"Where's your Mommy and Daddy?" Dawn asked the precarious child. "Would you like us to walk you home?" Dawn asked, while kneeling in front of her.

"I'm okay," the little girl lied, as Cheri did her part to help, by picking up the spilled candy off the ground and putting it back in the child's plastic pumpkin-shaped basket. "I don't live that far from here. I'll be fine," she nervously insisted.

Persephone took off running, as if her life were in dire jeopardy, in spite the fact that Dawn had been nothing but gentle and gracious.

"Just think of how she would have reacted if we had brought Wolf along," Cheri joked, trying to lighten things up, noticing Dawn's sadness in having unwittingly terrified the alarmed and malleable little girl.

As Dawn found herself forgetting her mission of revenge, she realized...much to her chagrin...that she wasn't making much of a dent in her quest to eradicate evil from America.

Meanwhile, four of the coven members are united at the Moon Lodge. They had gathered in a communal area, and had sprinkled the floor with red rose pedals. Red candles were lit and methodically placed around the room. Joy, Maria, Bonnie, and Sienna formed a circle, of which there were two mattresses inside. These bed cushions were also deliberately frosted with rose pedals. Incense burned, providing an aromatic blend of damiana, lavender, galangal root, cinnamon, vervain, patchouli, and powdered orris root. The girls were skyclad, which they always were for rituals such as this. They had assembled this time to invoke the Goddess and ask for her help in attracting Dawn, whom Joy was determined to coerce into surrendering and submitting to her carnal wishes. Joy had bathed herself in Aphrodite oil, to prepare for this certifiable ceremony.

They had just acknowledged the four elements and directions, and were now manually pleasuring themselves. The idea was that bringing themselves to climax would christen the room for the magick that was about to take place. The air was already thick and fume-infested, and now they were adding their estrogen perfume to the mix. As each of the young women fingered themselves with enthusiasm, Bonnie and Sienna both squirted as they came. Joy and Maria masturbated just as vigorously, but knew they weren't built with the same capacity, so they urinated on the floor after they made themselves cum. Joy recited an ancient incantation, which was meant to enforce Dawn to succumb to her desires and demands, despite her free will. Joy wanted the young squashim, and she would do everything in her dark power to capture Dawn's attention and snatch her up.

"O mighty Isis, who is goddess of the moon
Guardian of our beloved, whose blood flows in tune
We pour forth love on nature, as we dance
In your stead, I offer myself and beg for romance
With your Left Hand Path, please bless
The object of whom I wish to undress
Grant me this, so perfect peace I shall know
While resting in your hellish arms below
So that to serve both thee and me
I insist on this now, so mote it be

*That I shall rove, and get it quick and fast
As I will, this fucking spell is cast!"*

Joy reached for a goblet filled with spiked red wine, and walked it outdoors as she held it securely above her head, all the while continuing her persistent chanting to further forcefully influence Dawn's devoted affections. The three obedient, and inferior, witches followed their revered priestess into the vast garden out front. Joy holds the polluted chalice up to the moonlight, to energize the liquid contents. She does this for precisely nine minutes, then watches as the moon's reflection forms cryptic images on the fluid's surface.

"I invite you in, where you may never go. With me, you belong. I deem it so," Joy shouted, as her three sisters stood naked with her on the extravagantly deluxe, private property.

"Be cleansed of individuality and negativity. As we will, so mote it be," Bonnie added, while throwing up her arms, as another way of blatantly mocking the Christian way of worship.

"Gentle, subtle, obsidian stone, make her submit, help us bone," Maria contributed, before cackling in her own amusement.

"Potion of great power, which we hold in our face, flow with the Goddess, and now interlace. Your mighty sovereignty aids us in our plea. In the names of Isis and Crowley, so mote it be," the fair-skinned black beauty chimed in. Sienna's physical appearance was both alluring and disturbing. She had one green eye and the other brown, both of which were atypically bright and pastel in tint. Her eyebrows were joined, and her hair was prematurely gray for her youthful age, which followed suit with her unmatched, glassy eyes.

The four ladies took turns drinking from the drugged concoction, which included human blood, urine, and various hallucinogens and aphrodisiacs. They then laid down on the beds of rose pedals and engaged in uninhibited hedonism and debauchery, which would have been charming and winsome had they felt anything for each other, rather than doing it to celebrate their batshit and inimical plan.

After 90 minutes of pleasuring and satisfying each other with venereal delight, the four young women cuddled and snuggled on the stained mattresses. As they spooned one another, or rested their heads on each other's breasts, they noticed that they all smelled of fragrance that was distinctively bay leaf, mugwort, and nutmeg. This wasn't a perfume they had applied, but a natural scent that exuded from their pores. Joy's eyes turned the color of black onyx, just briefly, so it went unnoticed. Sienna, who appeared to be the other dominant one, felt her bi-colored eyes become like a multi-colored opal, but only momentarily. Sienna had the outline of a *Levi's* jeans pocket tattooed on her left butt cheek, which also made her hard to ignore.

Meanwhile, Agent Shelling found himself lost, dead in his tracks, and completely stumped on where to go or what to do next. Of course, he didn't have many options at this particular juncture. He leaned his back against his American-made *POS*, with the hood propped open and black smoke rising from the mediocre engine. His unreliable hunk of junk wasn't the only thing that was burned out. He was tired of going nowhere, getting nowhere, and having nobody. He wasn't so different from the troubled nephew that he was so hellbent on avenging. The distressed Federal agent had to consciously remind himself of his mission and make himself feel overwrought again, so he could keep his promise and bring Dawn down. He shared William's obsessive-compulsive habits, as he caught himself scrubbing and spit-shining the car that was currently on fire.

Joy sat on the edge of the jungle-themed deck, stressfully squeezing a bloodstone in her hand, battling doubt and disbelief in her own Satanic religion. She was alone at the moment, and clothed in nothing but a yellow tank top and matching yellow panties. She places a white candle beside her, but it's not an ordinary candle. It's made of human baby fat, instead of wax. Joy begins to pray another blasphemous prayer, begging for the Goddess to guide Dawn to her, even if it means bringing her harm in the process. Joy lights the wick, and says:

"Oh flame of Hades that burns so bright
Be a beacon on this hallowed night
Light the Path for our Indian fiend
That she embrace, which she's weened
Lead her into the Summerland
And shine until Isis takes her hand
And with your light, bring her to me
That she may rest and kill with glee"

Joy uses her thumb and index finger to snuff out the flame, and stares aimlessly into the top opening of the candle, as she takes in the aroma of roasted, infant flesh. She continued praying her abominable prayer, with this blood-curdling ending.

"Farewell, dear sun, who heats the earth
Who, with your light, brings joy and mirth
Close your eyes now, and go to sleep
Rest peacefully in darkness deep."

Cheri stands guard in the homeowner's driveway, while Dawn furiously drinks from the stranger's garden hose to quench her dehydration. Dawn feels as if she's suffering a heatstroke, and can't figure out the reason or the cause. The world begins to spin around her, as if she is sucked into a vortex that only she can see or feel. Lightheaded and frightened, she calls out for Cheri, and as she does, her words sound as if they aren't coming from her own mouth. Dawn looks up at the full moon and sees that it has turned red. She begins to lose her balance, as if the ground is quaking underneath her. Cheri chivalrously rushes up to her, to catch her and keep her from collapsing. As Cheri stops her fall and tenderly holds her, Dawn notices that her hair has now turned completely white, and wonders why Cheri isn't commenting on the drastic change. However, what Dawn couldn't see was that these were simply optical illusions, and merely a detour on her slow ride to the sea of madness. (Acts 2:20; Joel 2:31; Revelation 6:12) Dawn begins to cry, first softly, then loudly, making a scene for the surrounding trick-or-treaters and their parents.

"It's okay, sweetie," Cheri told her, trying her best to console her sobbing lover, having no clue what had provoked such a tantrum. "Hang in there, baby. Everything will be alright."

Agent Shelling was still stranded, still bogged down, and still burdened with stress. None of the passing vehicles had stopped in concern or offered any assistance. The derailed disaster had rubbed his totaled car with such zealous potency, that it actually left bare patches in the solvent-based paint. Agent Shelling found himself in a tumultuous frenzy, agitated and aggravated with the evasive tribal terrorist. He swore to the memory of his unhinged nephew, that he wouldn't accept dismal failure.

"This will not be my legacy!" the Federal agent told the late William, once again making promises he knew he couldn't keep. "I would rather kill myself than let this bitch get away with what she did to you!"

It was somewhere between midnight and the witching hour, and Cheri had finally gotten Dawn home. She was calm and sedated, purely due to the halfbreed's mind-control ability. Dawn was soon sprawled out on the bed, while Wolf whimpered for her. Cheri wasted no time laying on top of her, with her three nipples pressed up against Dawn's exposed chest. Cheri ravaged her, and relaxed her by kissing her neck with her forked tongue. She scratched Dawn's luscious figure with her sturdy nails, while leaving deep hickeys on her neck and breasts. Cheri had completely blindsided Dawn again with her supernatural spell, doing well at concealing her demonic origin. Though the pink-haired mystique didn't wish to cripple or maim Dawn anymore, as she had genuinely grown to love her, the very engagement of their sexual exchange continued to drain Dawn of her essence and vital energy.

"You look good enough to eat," the tattooed Cheri said, while staring into Dawn's blue eyes with her own special shade of blue. "I'll tell you what, baby. Why don't I return the favor?"

"Favor?" Dawn asked, unsure what she meant.

"Yeah. I feel bad that I made you eat me out while I was on the rag. So, why don't I make it up to you and drink a little of your blood? Think of it as a way of making us blood lovers. It will be an unbreakable bond that will tie us together for life, making us inseparable and our love eternal. I can't think of anything more romantic than that."

"We call that *Danitaga*," Dawn said.

Later that morning, after a peaceful sleep, they ate a chicken salad that had chunked *Goldrush* and *Fuji* apples, and tart, sliced lemons in the recipe. Cheri and Dawn went right back to bed after breakfast, falling asleep together, once again in endearing embrace. Dawn spooned her from behind at first, and later on rolled over on her other side. Cheri wound up lying flat on her back, with her arms crossed over her bare chest.

NOVEMBER 18, 1978
THE SNOW MOON

Unlike Linda had been, Dawn had no intention of being an absent or neglectful mother. On the same token, one could argue that she was focused on herself and her longing to be needed and desired again. Dawn hated leaving little Donnie outside, but trusted that Wolf would guard him with his life. Dawn was very lonely and willing to go to whatever lengths necessary to change that isolated status. She adored her baby boy, but she needed more. Being the mother to Reuben's child was everything, but wasn't enough. She needed the warmth and intimacy of romance again. Wolf was outside, watching over the little tike and living up to her expectations. He lied down in a way that cushioned and cradled the baby, to keep little Donnie snug and safe. Donnie attempted to break free a time or two, but whenever Wolf felt him try to crawl away, he blocked and pulled him back with his arm or claws, or used his teeth to gently lift him up and set him back down against his insulated fur. Dawn had dressed Donnie in a onesy that she had stitched out of padded leather, but Wolf wanted to ensure that he was kept as cozy as possible. Dawn was Wolf's friend, and her son was as important to him as if Donnie was his own cub. That was when Dawn woke from her dream, and remembered that her precious son was dead at birth and that she had a girlfriend. Wolf was outside, but only because he wasn't allowed admittance into the venue. The only reason why Wolf didn't scare anybody, was because all the fans were either stoned on arrival or too braindead to be heedful. Dawn was on a special date with her rosy-haired lesbian lover, which would prove to be an evening impossible to predict and the herald to a ruthless Winter.

It was a Saturday, and the very day that the *People's Temple* had been forced into a mass pseudo-suicide, in their oppressive, captive-community in Jonestown, Guyana. 900 cult members were horribly murdered earlier that afternoon, 300 of which had been children. As wicked and warped as Jim Jones was, he wasn't that different from every other preacher. While this religious massacre was disturbing news, it was too distant from the tragedy that was Dawn's existence. *Van Halen's* road crew were on stage, setting up for the band's opening act. While wannabe groupies were already ripping and tearing their tops off, in fandom anticipation to see *Black Sabbath*, Dawn was simply excited about the experience and grateful for the opportunity of seeing such a historical event. The *Chaparral Center* was packed, not leaving an empty seat in the auditorium. The versatile facility was located on the main campus of

Midland College, and accommodated a capacity of a 5,500 audience.

Nikolas Schreck and his Satanic girlfriend had just come from a ritualistic ceremony at the *Black House*, which was a single-family home that was moderately sized and entirely black (except for its brick staircase and small porch). The infamous house served as *The Church of Satan*, as well as one of Anton LaVey's multiple real estate properties. This San Francisco residence had also been the venue of the first recorded Satanic Baptism (in 1967), of which little Zeena was the recipient. Nikolas had brought Zeena to this concert performance in Midland, TX, to celebrate her turning fifteen that next day. They were casually chatting with a distinguished plutocrat named, Mathias, who had just sold them some exorbitant LSD. Dawn had boldly butted in, midway through the private conversation, as she was enthralled by how bewitching Zeena was.

"Are you Isis?" Dawn asked, smitten and mesmerized by Zeena's charismatic radiance, and mistaking her for the moon goddess she had previously learned about. Dawn flips out like an obsessive fangirl, while Cheri isn't thrilled with, or pleased by, her starstruck infatuation.

Dawn wasn't fond of fashionable cosmetics, but the Satanic princess wore it well and made it look good. Zeena had her share of make-up on her face, including (but not limited to) blue eyeshadow and drawn-on slanted eyebrows. Her hair was long, straight, and dyed. She projected a vibe that was dark and creepy, but Dawn was strangely attracted to Zeena's physical beauty and brand of mystery.

"Why did I carve up my ear?" Nikolas asked, in direct response to Dawn's curious and somewhat intrusive inquiry. "I carved it up to make a statement, a protest if you will. It's symbolic of how sick I am of having to listen to this Judeo-Christian mumbo jumbo…"

Nikolas was wearing a *Raschel* knit *shirt-suit*, which had a solid black Elvis-collar, and matching front panel that zippered down to the attached briefs. The shirt was nylon and polyester, which had half sleeves and a drop seat. His right ear was self-mutilated, but it wasn't sliced off (though his subsequent and ensuing fate would plan otherwise).

"What? On purpose?" Dawn asked, shocked and stumped in disbelief. "Why would you do that to yourself? Why, for Christ' sake?"

"I didn't do it for Christ' sake. There is no Christ. I did it to show my hatred for society and allegiance to Satan."

"So, you don't believe in Christ, but you believe in Satan?" Cheri asked. "How can you buy into one and not the other?"

"Satan isn't a person. Satan is an idea, or a symbol. We only think of him in the semantic sense. Satanism doesn't worship any fictional deity, but merely represents little things like individuality, non-conformism, self-indulgence, and rational free-thinking. Satanism has unjustly become synonymous with the diabolical. We don't believe that there is any good or evil. That's a ridiculous concept, constructed from perpetuated ignorance and Christian rhetoric. We don't believe in Christ, because we don't need him. We believe we are our own gods."

"When Eve took from the forbidden fruit, she became the first witch," Zeena continued, adding to her boyfriend's philosophy. "The tree of knowledge was witchcraft. God tried to hide this from us, because he knew we'd no longer need him if we could become our own gods and goddesses."

"Seriously? You wouldn't call what you did to your own ear, *evil*?" Cheri asked, not sure whether or not to interpret Nikolas as a brainwashed buffoon, or something else.

"Who's to say what's evil? Who are we to judge or label anything? That's just Christian indoctrination," Nikolas impudently proposed, while noticing Dawn visually admiring and mentally fucking his bleached-blonde girlfriend. "So, what brings you here?" he asked, turning his back on Cheri, and pitching his undivided attention in Dawn's direction.

"Who, me? Oh, um…I'm just here for the gig," Dawn answered him, even though his question regarded why she had imposed on their conversation rather than why she had come to the rock show.

"We're on a date," Cheri interceded, as she took a healthy sip of the Bloody Mary that she had initially bought for Dawn. Cheri had her hair partly up, set in a pastel pink banana clip, and wore a matching pink turtleneck under her purple leather vest, which was her version of dressing up. "Dawn and I are together. We're a couple," she clarified, in a mildly possessive tone.

"A couple of what?" Nikolas asked, insultingly, once again showing Cheri blatant disrespect.

"Are you a fan of the headliner?" Zeena asked a stupid question, completely ignoring Cheri's obvious jealousy and Nikolas's audacious sarcasm. The blonde beauty wanted to cross-examine Dawn, as she got a strong vibe that there was more to her than met the eye…and could vividly see her dark aura.

"You bet," she answered, blushing over Zeena's returned attention. Dawn was a bit confused as to why she was finding another girl so irresistibly appealing. Cheri had captured her heart, but evidently hadn't monopolized it. Dawn wondered if she had completely switched teams, sexually speaking. She observed that Nikolas had taken notice of her flirting and didn't approve, but she didn't care. Dawn had grown numb to many things, including what others thought of her. Little did she know that Zeena's ostensible charisma would prove to be superficial and soon be overshadowed by Cheri's devotion.

"Well, it certainly seems to be a full house," Nikolas said, clearing his throat as he notices that Zeena not only doesn't mind Dawn's concupiscence, but seems to be reciprocating her looks of lechery. "It's a sold-out show," he said again, trying to get his girlfriend's focus back on the rock concert, or on him. Neither Cheri or Dawn thought much of Nikolas, as he came across as a snobbish hipster who arrogantly thought he knew everything about everything, which wasn't exactly a turn-on.

Van Halen began performing their new single, *Runnin' With the Devil*, as those still standing found their seats. Mathias had left the group discussion awhile ago, but no one had discerned him walking away or missing.

"Come on, baby. We should find our seats?" Cheri suggested to Dawn, jumping right in and fighting the lame lines and phony courtship between Dawn and Zeena. Dawn didn't want to leave, but the bleached-blonde Satanist nodded her head, smiled, and winked at her admirer, before Nikolas escorted her to their own assigned seating.

Cheri and Dawn found their seats, which were clear on the other side of the stadium from where Zeena and Nikolas were reserved. "Do you believe in kismet?" Cheri asked, once they sat down. The moment they got settled in, faces in the crowd began to rise to their feet. The opening act had turned out to be a pleasant surprise, as they immediately won the audience over, nailing every tune and killing it on stage.

Cheri had dressed particularly nice for this special outing with Dawn, and had even loaned Dawn a pair of her flowered linen trousers, which looked even better on Dawn's hips and firm ass. Despite vicious rumors and popular belief, Cheri didn't let just anyone get into her pants. They say that a dog is *man's best friend*, but Cheri would eventually come to disagree with that. Not that Dawn was a dog...far from in fact...but Cheri saw the animal in her, and was certain that the beast side of Dawn was what had truly fascinated Zeena's mutual attraction.

Dawn was struck speechless by her *kismet* question, and didn't know what to say in response. Cheri's hair was much lighter than her departed ginger-lover, but her heart wasn't that different from his, if you could overlook that she was half-demon. Her crystal-blue eyes seemed to pierce straight through Dawn's broken, hardened heart like an arrow from *Cupid* himself. Dawn saw Cheri as this flawless specimen of extraordinary delight, which was a first-sight feeling that was returned and shared by the salacious pink lady. People danced where they stood, moving and grooving to *Van Halen's* set. Wolf dug the music too, as he could hear it clear as day, from the packed parking lot. Dawn and Cheri both remained seated, content with listening to the music and looking at each other.

"I like your hemp bracelet," she said in compliment, which was the only thing that Dawn was able to verbalize just then, hoping to change the subject. "It goes really nice with all your rings." Cheri's bracelet had a centerpiece of turquoise, which was eye-catching as well.

"Do you like hemp?" she asked Dawn, smiling at her and playing along. "Are you cool?"

"I like to think I'm hip," Dawn answered, smiling back.

"Yes, you are," Cheri agreed, while glancing down at Dawn's hourglass figure, and subconsciously staring at the coveted area between her legs. Dawn was wearing her tribal bone choker, which definitely clashed with her glittery outfit. She wore a silvery top that tied around both her back and neck, which revealed much of her cleavage, her midriff, and her smooth shoulders. Dawn had an appetizing tummy, but tasted even better below the belt, which was a fact that did not escape or go unappreciated by Cheri. Dawn's abdominal and pubic hair still had not grown back.

"Can I ask you something?" Cheri asked.

"Of course," Dawn said back, as she swallowed uncomfortably and hoped that it wasn't a marriage proposal, not that marrying a woman would have been a legal option.

"Do you think I'm a drag?" Cheri asked, trying her best to hide her hurt feelings from seeing Dawn suddenly act so detached.

"Drugs expand your mind," Mathias told Dawn, sneaking up behind them and unknowingly saving her by his rude interruption. He was a dark figure that was well hidden, but hard to miss. He wore a black top hat, and a black suit that was accessorized with a red cape. Dawn could see his face, but she'd soon wish to forget it. He, on the other hand, had no desire to stop seeing hers in his unhinged head. "Are you open to expanding your mind?" he aggressively asked her, with more than one meaning behind his intrusive question.

"Sure," Dawn said. "I'm open to anything."

Mathias completely spurned Cheri's presence for no valid reason, then tries to persuade Dawn into agreeing to swap sexual favors with him for a bag filled with the narcotic of her choosing. Dawn just gave Cheri a look, and they both smiled and laughed in comical amusement, while showing the drug pusher that she wasn't interested by not even acknowledging his illicit and unprepossessing proposition. Mathias, though humiliated with aspersions, accepted temporary defeat and walked away.

***

The high-profile concert seemed to have flown by, as the loud show was over before they knew it. Zeena pinpointed them and followed Cheri and Dawn outside, during *Black Sabbath's* roaring finale, and saw Wolf waiting there patiently and peacefully in the lawn. The moment that Wolf saw Dawn come out of the doors, he perked up, leapt to his feet, and ran up to greet her. Like an overgrown puppy, he stood on his hind legs and licked her face clean, as if they had been apart for a few months instead of a few hours.

"Is that your familiar?" Zeena inquired, genuinely interested.

"Familiar?" Dawn asked. "That's the second time I've heard that word used in this way. Are domesticated wolves that common?"

"You're adorable," she responded, tittering under her breath. "No, a *familiar* is what we witches call spirit animals. Is he yours?" Zeena asked.

"I'm not sure he's anyone's?" Dawn answered honestly. "He's my friend."

"I totally get that," Zeena told her. "We hold animals in high regard, despite the unfounded hysteria you hear about us sacrificing them, which is an idea that is just offensive and detestable to us. When I was a child, my closest friend was a lion. We grew up together. So, yeah, I get it," Zeena said, smiling at her, as she reached out and stroked the back of Wolf's head. "He's beautiful."

Dawn and Cheri were equally stunned that Wolf let Zeena pet him, which was unusual for him to trust a person so quickly. They couldn't deny, though, that Zeena had a hypnotic magnetism about her, which was no less than mesmerizing.

"If you're not doing anything," Zeena began, "why don't you come and hang out with my boyfriend and I? The night's still young," she invited, smiling warmly at Dawn. "Maybe we'll sit around a campfire somewhere and sing *Kumbayah*?"

"Kumbayah?" Nikolas said, overhearing too little of Zeena's tempting invite. "Is that some kind of Indian food?"

The prospect of spending more time with Zeena enchanted Dawn, but she couldn't help but notice what her excitement was doing to Cheri.

"I can't, Zeena. I'm sorry," Dawn respectfully declined, as she reached out and took Cheri's soft and shaky hand into hers. "I appreciate the kind offer, and am very flattered, but my loyalties are with Cheri."

"It's fine," Cheri lied, with her head hanging and her eyes focused on the asphalt beneath her. "Don't let me hold you back. If you want to go, I'll understand. It's okay."

Dawn squeezed her hand, while rubbing the outside with her thumb. "Baby," she said, "look at me." Dawn used her free hand to lift up Cheri's chin. The raspberry woman tried to avert her eyes, as if trying to hold back the outbreak of emotion. "Cheri, my heart soars like a hawk. I don't want to go. I'm where I belong…with you."

Cheri, though pleased with Dawn's endearing decision, couldn't stomach the guilt that was eating at her. So, as Zeena walked away, she chose to come clean about her being a semi-succubus, and having had manipulated Dawn for her own selfish benefits. She told Dawn that she was orphaned at birth, because her mother couldn't physically handle her delivery. Even though she was raised by the state, and never knew her father, she began to notice certain things about herself as she developed. Not only could she could hurt people, just by a touch or a thought, but by doing so…it would give her strength and even cure whatever ailed her. She could hear sinister voices from the other side, encouraging her to use and harm others. She was also able to see people for what they really were, under the surface. If she passed a sociopath on the street, she could see them as monsters with fangs, horns, and claws.

"So, do you see me that way?" Dawn asked her. "Do you see me as a monster?" Dawn momentarily daydreamed about her mother having been regularly absent, and her preacher father habitually doing things to her while he thought she was asleep. Rev. Mingan had once told her that there was nothing sinister under her bed or in her closet, because *monsters didn't exist*.

"No," Cheri answered honestly, "I don't. Not at all." This was precisely what she still couldn't understand about Dawn. When she looked at her, she didn't see her as a murderous shapeshifter, even though Cheri had finally figured out that that's exactly what she was. "You're not evil, Dawn. You're broken, and you're angry, but you're not evil. Sociopaths are monsters who get their joy from hurting others, and usually target those whom they pretend to love for a time, like these Country wives who secretly use their husbands for babies or profit. When they're done with their trusting victims, they throw the poor fools away, leaving them betrayed and ruined. You're not capable of any of that. You have a heart that's genuine and that feels. You feel so much, and so intensely, that it's led you to kill. But, you only kill the body, not the soul. You're not evil, Dawn. You're not a monster."

"But, you are," Dawn said, basing her judgment on what Cheri had just revealed about herself. Dawn loved Cheri, but was taken aback by discovering that her sensitive and sensual lover was really an infernal scoundrel.

"Dawn, I need you to know that you mean everything to me. I never imagined that someone could kindle my stagnant heart the way you have." As Cheri confessed to her original and dishonorable intentions, she hung her hopes on Dawn accepting her extended olive branch and granting her the second chance she so craved, but not so much deserved. Cheri did something then, which she never thought possible. She wept. Not only did she cry, but her tears flowed like the Nile and stung like a scorpion's bite.

Dawn, shocked and appalled, impulsively deserted both Cheri and Wolf. She chased after Zeena, catching her and Nikolas as they were driving away in their black 1976 *Plymouth* Feather Duster, leaving Cheri stranded and sad, but guilt-free. Boston's, *More Than A Feeling*, blares over the car stereo as Nikolas and Zeena whisk Dawn away from Cheri's embrace…and Wolf's endearing adoration and codependency. Wolf looks up at Cheri and whimpers, as if to warn her that he can't survive without Dawn, so he runs after her to no avail, until he eventually gives up and watches the embodiment of his heart fade into the darkness. Though Cheri's intentions were good, and her heart was now in the right place, her disconcerting confession inadvertently pushed Dawn away. Unlike most romantic relationships, theirs had never suffered any illogical conflict. When they were together, Dawn's spiritual emanation would range between purple, red, and pink, but her feelings never fluctuated. There was a real connection there between them, and Cheri didn't wish to see it end.

A strange man walks up to Cheri. "Are you okay?" he asks, observing that she looks pale and lost.

"Anyone who tells you that *love isn't pain*, is either a fabricator or has never been in love. Whoever tells you that *time heals all*, is also selling you something," Cheri shared, while her broken heart practically pounded right through her tight chest, as she already missed her insatiable lover and felt the agony and misery of their separation.

"Find what you love and let it kill you," he told her. "I believe a famous poet once said that, though I could be wrong. I usually am."

The recent Top 40 hit, *Please Don't Leave*, by Lauren Wood, is booming and playing from one of the many motor vehicles patiently waiting to leave the jammed parking lot. As she heard Michael McDonald serving as the backing vocals to the *Warner Bros'* recording artist, her eyes refilled with tears as she wished she had been born heterosexual. She sits frozen in her van, too wrecked and weakened to even turn the key in the ignition. Wolf is equally shattered, as he smells and sniffs the passenger seat where Dawn once occupied. Even though Cheri had initially been the one to set the booby trap, Dawn became the one holding the upper hand in the end. Cheri's original intentions had been malicious and toxic, but now this same partial succubus found herself torn between her demonic roots and her unplanned, unexpected love for Dawn.

Hours later, Dawn finds herself partying hard with Zeena and Nikolas at one of Mathias's many homes.

Once she realized where her new friends had taken her, she initially felt understandably awkward, until the Satanic host showed her that he didn't hold a grudge. At least, that was the way the hospitable guru made it appear. Joy, Maria, and Bonnie are there, among nine other young women. Once again, they are all dressed in those uniform yellow hoodies that expose their perfect abdomens. One of the girls, Harriet, had a chronic skin condition that made her abnormally susceptible to carcinoma, so she stayed indoors.

Each one of the girls had a dark secret or unique condition, which made them easy prey for a cult leader like Mathias. Like Crowley, his mentoring predecessor, Mathias had been endowed with a plethora of luxurious properties, all funded by his inherited trust fund and the generous monetary contributions, donations, and sacrifices of his naive and obedient female disciples.

This particular dwelling, which was built more like a compound, had a disco room with a lighted dance floor that was accentuated with flickering colored squares and a mirrored ceiling. There was also an indoor Olympic-sized swimming pool, which was accompanied by a *Jacuzzi*, all with marble tiles and stone floors. There was also a roller rink, equipped with an on-site deejay and an impressive record collection. All of this, of course, were merely a few groovy aspects of this trendy masterpiece of a domicile.

As colossally enormous as the plantation was, it only had one bedroom in the entire compound. The bedroom was the size of six bedrooms and had three King-size beds all laid out beside each other, with three plush sofas to go along with them. The massive room was covered in bright green, patterned wallpaper. The inside of the closet is lined with patterned wallpaper that combines shades of bright green, yellow, black, and white. This bedroom also included an altar, which served as a shrine to Dawn. She hadn't seen this, as they still had Dawn on a probation period, where they were trying to decide whether or not she could be trusted.

The living area was decked out in shades of brown and beige, and included an eye-catching, bright green, circular couch that was the same shade as the six imposing chairs arranged around a mirror table in the dining room.

The equally groovy kitchen is decorated with patterned wallpaper that combines shades of turquoise, beige, and yellow, in trademark psychedelic shapes. It's an eat-in kitchen, complete with a table and chairs, as well as a large walk-in pantry.

Vintage bottles of perfume are lined on the shelves of the two bathrooms. These bathrooms both brought a pop of orange to the commune, along with touches of dark and light grey.

Then, there was the heated garage and equally immeasurable outdoor parking space, along with a runway, a private jet, and a crop farm where Mathias often put the girls to work.

Mathias had a septagram tattooed on the web of his left hand. This seven-pointed sigil was what the witches called a *faery star*, which was sacred to the late *Beast* (Aleister Crowley). The perverted and deranged sorcerer wore red-lensed sunglasses that were round shaped. His circular glasses were designed to give the illusion that he was saluting the king of the hippies, but in reality, it was an insult meant to defame, degrade, and disparage the former *Beatle*. The all-female coven walked around with nothing on below their waist. Dawn couldn't help but notice the branding on each of their left butt cheeks, which was a unicursal hexagram that was the equivalent of the Egyptian ankh. It was as if these girls were owned, like cattle. The only member who didn't bare this symbol was Sienna, only because her left cheek already showcased the tattooed outline of the *Levi's* jeans pocket.

"Naked is sacred," he tells Dawn, noticing her staring at the other girls, who have their crop hoodies on, and only their crop hoodies on. Magus Mathias wore a long yellow dress, which looked more like a drape. One would normally see this and presume that he was gay, but considering the way he drooled over her and treated his followers, Dawn knew otherwise and never doubted his sexuality for a minute. He was clearly just eccentric, and perhaps a tad flamboyant, but certainly not homosexual. "My real name is Alexei Sirieus," he confided in her, hoping she would appreciate his honesty, and maybe even open herself up to him in return. "It's a German name, and can be a tongue-twister for some people, so I changed it. Besides, *Magus Mathias* sounds more like a spiritual leader, don't you think?"

What the fanatical guru didn't reveal to Dawn was that he had been severely maltreated as a child, which would become a pivotal factor in him becoming a sinister savage. Before he would come to be the charismatic pseudanor, he had a damaging history of being bullied, rejected, and made to wear a pink dress and smeared lipstick…and that was from his church leaders. This, however, failed to turn him queer, but rather motivated him to use religion as a slick way to manipulate and molest as many jailbait women as possible. *The Golden Veil* coven called him *Mathias*, but also referred to him as *Master Vaingory*, especially during certain ceremonies and selective rituals.

Mathias gives Dawn moonshine, which she immediately indulges and gorges herself with to make up for lost time. She gulps the heavy, fiery liquor down her throat, as if it were water and she was dying from dehydration, while Mathias talks her ear off. Little did he know that she wasn't paying any attention to his rants and ramblings. Even when she'd take a break from her appeased alcoholism, she couldn't give him her undivided concentration, as she was too focused on and distracted by his other tattoo, which was even more appalling and revolting than the one on his hand. He had the number *666* tattooed on the center of his forehead, just above his eye level. His eyebrows were also completely shaved off, which made his appearance look even more bizarre and macabre. This diabolical and blasphemous number was intended to pay homage to his unhealthy obsession with the decayed, Aleister Crowley. Mathias wore an amulet, hanging over his chest, which was a triangle that had a small circle on its tip, with a horizontal crescent moon resting on top.

The Buzzcocks tune, *Ever Fallen In Love (With Someone You Shouldn't've)*, comes on, playing from one of the phonographic records from Mathias's extensive, near-mint collection of LPs. This doesn't help Dawn's current heartbreak, as the UK lyrics only further remind her of Cheri, who wasn't as easy to walk away from as she had made it seem. The punk song was about loving someone who was clearly bad for you, but being terrified of losing them and living without them. Zeena noticed her slouching on the green sofa with her face in her hands, as Mathias hovered over her like a dark cloud. Zeena took Nikolas by the hand and led him to the couch, whether he wanted to come with or not. As soon as they joined Dawn on the sofa, Mathias took his silent cue and stepped away.

"Are you okay?" Zeena asked, while tenderly rubbing her back. "Can we do something for you? Can *I* do something for you?" she asked, while delicately throwing herself at her, just in case Dawn wanted to use her body to soothe her sorrows. Nikolas sat on the other side of Dawn, rolling his eyes and not nearly as attentive or nurturing as his bleached-blonde girlfriend.

"Cheri had an agenda all along," Dawn said, sobbing softly, as she confided in Nikolas and Zeena about what the culpable Cheri had told her in strict confidence. "I trusted her, and she was a fucking chameleon. I'm so stupid. I should have known something was wrong. Whenever we would make love, I would feel sick afterwards, like she had stolen my health." Dawn leaned to her side and let Zeena cradle her against her bosom. Zeena wore a fairly tight and revealing blouse, and no bra, so Dawn's head got to feel the blunt of her bust. This would have turned her on, had she not been so traumatized and fractured over learning Cheri's dark secret. Zeena stroked her hair and fondled her scalp, while Dawn cried into her welcoming and underage chest.

"There are no psychic vampires," Nikolas declared, trying to refute his Machiavellian, future father-in-law who had coined the term. Cheri wasn't an energy vampire, but he assumed she was, based on the evidence that she possessed some of the same characteristics. "There are no good vampires, just as there are no white witches. Don't believe in all that contemporary Wiccan bullshit, because that's all it is. You are what you are, and if your personality is counterfeit and used to deceive others, you're a fraud and a hypocrite and I can't condone or respect that."

"It just stings," Dawn said, weeping softly. "I opened up to her. I let her in. She's an animal. Part of me wants to forgive her, but I don't know if I can?"

"We don't believe in forgiveness," Zeena shared. "Jesus taught his followers to turn the other cheek, but if you live by that proverb, sooner or later you run out of cheeks," she told Dawn, as she wiped away her tears with her soft hand. "There is no redemption for maltreatment, but only retribution."

"Zeena grew up with a pet lion," Nikolas repeated what Zeena had previously shared with her. "The Bible talks about Daniel being in the lion's den and what a miracle it was that God saved him from being devoured by the bloodthirsty beasts, but there was no miracle in that. Lions, and the animal kingdom in general, are naturally more benevolent than most human beings. Humans are the *real* animals."

Sienna brings over a serving tray and offers Dawn a cup of Chai tea. The tray, pitcher, and the cup are all made from sandalwood. The tea has infused chamomile and patchouli leaves as a garnish. There is a pair of mint candies that sit on the tray as well, as an after-refreshment. Dawn politely declines, but Sienna can't hear her, as she is legally deaf. She stares at Dawn with her ghastly look, making her feel awkward and nervous. Sienna's *Waardenburg Syndrome* is hard to look at, even for Dawn. Her dual-colored eyes, which are widely spaced, make Dawn uncomfortable. The herbal blend smells like lemon-flavored catnip. Zeena gives the light-skinned gothic girl a look, which lets her know that Dawn isn't interested and is already taken care of.

"You should've taken the black tea," the Satanic princess told Dawn. "It relaxes the mind and opens you up to receiving divinely-guided messages and visions." As Zeena heard herself giving this advice, she remembered that she was talking to an American Indian, who likely needed no help in that department. She continued petting Dawn's pretty head, as another bottomless girl approached them.

"Would you like an appetizer?" Gwenn offered, holding a different, but similar, wooden tray of finger food. "Perhaps avocado dip and pretzels, or a nice orange peel?"

"Guinevere!" Joy yelled over the music, calling Gwenn Gates by her witch name. "Leave Dawn alone! She doesn't want any!" Embarrassed, Gwenn bowed to Dawn, as if giving an unspoken apology, then humbly walked away in humiliation.

"You should try the wine here," Nikolas recommended, as Zeena's hands change course and begin to explore Dawn's body, first over the clothes, then under. "The girls always spice it perfectly with cinnamon and basil."

Dawn, in her vulnerable state, doesn't fight Zeena's aggressive moves, but instead gives into their mutual yearning for one another. This leads to heavy petting, fierce kissing, and passionate facesitting, which all take place right there on the couch, in front of everyone. Dawn's clothes were easier for Zeena to take off, than it was for Dawn to get Zeena out of her snug, black leather pants. The daughter of American Satanism smothers Dawn's pretty face with her juicy ass, spreading her butt cheeks to give the Cherokee easier access to her neighboring holes, as Dawn vigorously rimmed Zeena's brown eye and thoroughly cleaned her wet pussy with her eager tongue. Zeena's cunt tasted as sweet as sugar, but she was a wolf of an entirely different breed. Though Nikolas doesn't approve, he joins in on the voyeurism as a closeted cuckhold, which overpowers his feelings of pride and jealousy. Zeena reciprocated Dawn's avid diligence by leaving love bites and bruises all over her body, with her audaciously assertive chewing and sucking. Zeena didn't mind Dawn's body hair, but actually found it arousing. Zeena was very fond of animals, and Dawn was certainly bringing the animal out in her. This was quite evident, since Dawn's abdominal and pubic hair had begun growing back rather quickly and suddenly, after a time of being nonexistent, and it appeared to be solely attributed to Zeena's influence and attention.

Hours later, the party is still going strong, well into the morning after. The Eagles' song, *Witchy Woman,* begins to play, as Dawn casually shuffles through Mathias's vinyl collection of LPs, many of which are by *The Doors.* Dawn's body is still sore from playing with Zeena, but the pleasure had far outweighed the pain, and she knew she would heal as she always did. Mathias sees Dawn going through his record collection and immediately perceives it as rifling. He walks over to her, not just to ensure that she doesn't steal, but to once again try in vain to win her over. Dawn looks at the covers for the albums, *Face the Music,* by ELO; *Dark Side of the Moon,* by Pink Floyd; *The Second Annual Report,* by Throbbing Gristle; and *Blood on the Snow,* by Coven. She even finds one or two 7-inch singles, including, *House of the Rising Sun,* by The Animals. Mathias can tell that she's still on the edge of a total meltdown, and can see her hands trembling from the unstable combination of hurt and anger. Zeena had certainly been a relaxing distraction, but that refreshing exchange could never begin to replace what she felt for Cheri. Dawn tried to pretend that she had moved on, but she knew better and couldn't deny who was in her heart. Dawn wasn't the type to *let go* of someone she loved, which was just one of the many ways she was different from most people.

"*Love* and *life* are both four-letter words," Mathias tried to convince her that she was better off discarding Cheri, since love is more often a curse rather than a blessing, which Dawn was admittedly beginning to agree with. "Damaged attracts damaged, unfortunately. Don't allow this disappointment to germinate in the soil of your heart." He laid his left hand on her shoulder as he told her this, which she wasted no time in shrugging off. However, he did take it as a good sign that she submitted to wearing one of the zippered yellow hoodies, although she insisted on wearing a pair of yellow panties to go with it. So, she was still playing hard to get, but he could tell that she was coming along...slowly but surely. He was making progress, or so he thought, which he was significantly pleased to watch and witness.

The fundamental pastor from the Pentecostal church is there. He's wearing a polyester jacket and his hair is stylishly permed. Dawn recognizes him, as she watches him lounge lazily on the couch, snorting coke, and getting felacio from an underage prostitute. There were other very young whores in other rooms of the compound, who were shamelessly cheating on their trusting boyfriends, devoted fiancees, and loving husbands. The perverted preacher laughed to himself, not just high on the dope he was ingesting, but also from the smoke stacks of secondhand toxins that were infecting the pagans and burn-outs who had been invited to this hedonistic bash.

"What?" he asked her, noticing her rude stare. "Do you want to taste this, too?" he crudely offered, referring to his phallic wand. "Is it your birthday too, doll? What's your sign? Come here then. Come to the witch doctor. Make a wish and blow," he arrogantly and obscenely propositioned her, not recognizing Dawn from visiting him before at his sham-of-a-church.

"Shouldn't you be wearing your cross?" Dawn asked him.

"The cross was originally a symbol of sadness," he said to the young Dawn, "and brought tragedy to those who wore it. It was also a symbol of mockery, not praise or respect, which shows you that Christians don't know their Bible. Now, why don't you come over here, little girl? Let's get freaky." Dawn was one of many who couldn't figure out Nikolas's age. He looked older than his statutory girlfriend, but nobody knew by how much. She would have asked him, but he creeped her out. Dawn also didn't wish to upset Zeena.

"You're the minister from that non-denominational…" she began aloud, calling him out for the despicable fraud he was. Little did she expect that he wouldn't flinch from being exposed or even attempt to deny his professional identity. He did, however, notice the evil eye she was giving him.

"What's a matter, baby?" he interrupted, while clearing his throat and beginning to second guess whom he was actually dealing with. "You look like you're demon possessed."

"Demonic possession is a falsehood," Nikolas suddenly cuts in, as he sneaks up from behind and lays his hands on Dawn's shoulders. "We are in control, not the demons."

"You never answered my question," Dawn reminded the minister.

While this pointless discourse launches between these two, Mathias has isolated himself in one of the few vacant rooms, looking over a special gift that he had earlier sent one of his girls to purchase. He had learned through the grapevine that Dawn had lost a valued flask that meant a great deal to her, and that she particularly had an affinity for silver. Mathias was formerly an Assistant Pastor of the London-based temple, *The Process Church of the Final Judgment*, but he renounced established religion and branched out on his own to start a new movement, in which he was the master and lord. His lucrative leadership in New Orleans, San Francisco, and Midland had made him ridiculously rich, so he could afford to buy Dawn whatever fancied her.

"You are as bitching as the fertile mother," the perverted preacher acknowledged her, while swallowing nervously and kissing her ass. "That's just a gig to pay the bills. I get a full offering plate every week and tax free status. Why wouldn't I do this for a living?" he asked, boastful and proud of his criminal sacrilege.

"You're a monster," she confronted him.

"God is the monster, my scary little hussy. The lamb has seven horns and seven eyes. Revelation speaks of four creatures in paradise, who bear the heads of a calf, a lion, an eagle, and a man, who are each full of eyes and wings. Talk about monsters. God demanded animal sacrifices in the Old Testament, and even had Isaac nearly murdered by his father, just because he could. Think about that for a minute…believers brutally and willingly slaughtered their pets and livestock, as well as their children, to cleanse themselves of sin that wasn't even sin. Yet, Satanists are the ones who allegedly butcher kids and animals, when it's they who hold these precious gems as sacred. God put Job through hell, just to win a bet. God is a narcissist. Everything he does is to abuse his power and boost his own ego."

LSD and cocaine are being passed around on an 11"x14" mirror. Some of the guests had finally begun to fall asleep, right where they were, be it on the floor or on furniture. Those who were still awake, were stoned out of their minds. Mathias wanted to get her sedated, but Dawn wasn't going to fall prey to his vices or wiles. She was gradually becoming lethargic, but it was going to take a major distraction for her to let down her guard. This is where the new flask would come in to play, but he couldn't give it to her quite yet. This piece of silver needed to be primed and modified first, before placed into her hungry hands. Mathias was moonstruck over Dawn, on an obsessive level. Like his submissive apostle, Joy, he could see Dawn for what she was, and it aroused him in a way he had never before felt. He desired her with an unrelenting lust that extended far beyond prurient hunger, and he would have her, whatever the cost. She had rejected his sexual advances every time, so using magick to lower her wall of defense was his only option.

"Goodbye, sweet Dawn," Zeena bid, after kissing her passionately on the mouth and then ever so gently on the forehead.

"You're leaving?!" Dawn asked, naive in thinking that Zeena was going to stay with her, or at the very least take her with them.

"Yes, my beautiful. Nikolas and I are expected home in California," she replied nonchalantly, as Nikolas opened wide the front door for his seductive 15-year-old girlfriend.

Dawn felt sad and used, as she hurried to think of anything that she could say or do to make Zeena not go, or invite her to go with them. "What if I became a Satanist too?" she asked in sheer desperation, not thinking about what she was actually offering or suggesting.

"Aww, baby, that's precious, but not possible," Zeena said, in a condescending tone, while giving her one last hug.

"One can't be converted into Satanism. It doesn't work that way. Our theology isn't like the patriarchal religions. Satanists are born, not made," Nikolas explained, without an ounce of decency or hint of sensitivity.

Zeena and Nikolas return to San Francisco, leaving Dawn in Mathias's wicked but capable hands, somehow convincing her to stay with him and his loose disciples at his mammoth home in Midland. Zeena and Nikolas would later form the Satanic gospel band, *Radio Werewolf*, in 1984, in Los Angeles, inspired in part by meeting Dawn that night in 1978. This band would grow to build a cult following, both in California and in Europe. Zeena would later wed Nikolas in 1988. They continued to operate *The Werewolf Order* (a school of Black Magick that ran from 1988-1999), though disbanded the musical collective in 1993. High Priestess, Zeena, would establish the *Sethian Liberation Movement* on November 8, 2002. Nikolas was obsessed with idolizing Charles Manson, sympathizing with him for taking the blame for crimes that weren't technically his fault. Photos of *Spahn Ranch* were often used in the band's artwork, which was one of their regular tour stops. He and Zeena would live to have a happy and lasting marriage, and settle in Berlin, Germany. The couple would renounce *The Left Hand Path* in 1990, and convert to Tantric Buddhism.

DECEMBER 21, 1978
YULE
WINTER SOLSTICE

John Wayne Gacy (aka: *The Killer Clown*) was finally arrested by the Chicago PD, after they blatantly ignored several red flags to Gacy's guilt. He had raped and murdered at least 33 teenage boys, most of whom would have been spared and prevented, had the apathetic authorities not shown such gross neglect.

As the Christmas holiday approaches, Mathias celebrates by having another drug-induced party at his compound. All twelve girls in *The Golden Veil* were accounted for. One of the visiting witches, Bethany Boyd, was busy in the kitchen baking festive cookies, among other diabetic treats. The compound smelled of chamomile, rosemary, and gingerbread. They had officially adopted Dawn as one of their clan, and had chosen to give her the pet name, *Lola*, which meant *sorrow*. Joy wanted to name her *Pandora*, but Mathias disagreed and had the final word. Dawn still refused to walk around without anything on below the waist. If she had been anybody else, she wouldn't have gotten away with such mutiny, but she received special treatment due to the fact that both Joy and Mathias wanted her…in more ways than one.

As usual, nobody would want for anything at Mathias's place, as he made certain that all had their greedy lusts met and tended to. Great copulations and orgies permeated the fleshy incense that consumed the many rooms. No sinful taboo would go unturned, and no forbidden fantasy would be denied. Joy was clothed in a *Boho Tan* jacket, but the rest of the coven wore the usual uniform yellow hoodies and nothing else. The quilted jacket actually belonged to Mathias, while Joy was the exceptional favorite who got to share its exclusive privilege. She was the High Priestess, and Mathias's left hand. Joy, however, would soon have some tough competition, if he had anything to say about it. Mathias fancied Dawn, and had big plans for her, whether she consented or not.

Maria Katsos was there with her mystifying pupils of jade. Bonnie Brooks was there, along with Melissa Miller, Michelle Gardocki (aka *Scarlet*), Emily Bryant (aka *Jezebel*), Roxanne Sivak (aka *Nebula*), Taylor Marie Feld (aka *Sadie*), Gwenn Gates, Crystal Renee Jump, and Sienna McDonald (aka *Ravyn*). *Scarlet* had several rings on her left hand, which she slid on as seasonal ornaments. She wore blue sunstone, emerald, ruby, and sapphire stones. Dawn looked at Michelle's decorated hand and felt her heart rise to the back of her throat, as she desperately and deeply missed Cheri. She knew she had made a horrible mistake in leaving her, and was really beginning to feel the realities and repercussions of regret.

The karaoke machine was hooked up, and Joy (aka *Danika*) was front and center, doing her best to belt out one of her favorite songs. However, as conniving and confident as she was off stage, she was somehow incapable of showing that same brass on the microphone. She was singing, *Friend Of The Devil*, by Grateful Dead, but you would never know it because no one could hear her. The queen of deceit and destruction had suddenly become a shy introvert, which marveled everyone, but relinquished no ridicule.

The party soon relocated to the heated swimming pool, where many of the residents and guests were skinny-dipping. Those who weren't playing in the water, were engaging in other watersports that were both degrading and defiling. As expected, there was no denying each other fulfillment, no matter how dark or depraved the fantasy. The words *repression* and *deprivation* weren't even in their vocabulary, and were considered forbidden within the optimistically safe walls of the compound and the unspoken regulations of the coven.

A couple of girls juggled fire balls, while another played with the fire in her hands, all without any protection, precaution, or prevention, and yet...not one of them were burned or harmed in any way, or on any level. Dawn noticed a young Hispanic teenager, who didn't appear to be a part of *The Golden Veil*, but who was equally as dark and disturbing. This girl was levitating above the hot tub, sitting in a lotus position while floating in the air; giving a whole new definition to the term, *Spanish Fly*.

Dawn suddenly felt the urge to have a *Dad's* Old Fashioned Cream Soda (subconsciously missing Reuben's semen), but Mathias didn't have any in stock, so *Sadie* came hurrying over with a tray. She had a Kool Aid *Goofy Grape* pitcher that was filled with water. The tray also had an empty glass, and a pouch of Root Beer flavored *Fizzies*. Taylor poured from the Funny Face *Pillsbury* pitcher into the block glass, which was decorated with orange and yellow squares. She then popped out two of the eight sparking soft drink tablets from the tinfoil package, and dropped them into the drinking glass. As Dawn watched the tablets dissolve in the water, like *Alka-Seltzer*, she began to feel faint. Her vision began to turn blurry and she could sense a tingling in her hands. A cold chill overcame her and she could feel someone breathing on the back of her neck, though there was nobody behind her that she could see.

Dawn felt her life force being fed on again, as if an unseen presence was absorbing her energy. Suddenly, Cheri was there…or at least her apparition…standing in front of Dawn, who was sitting in a funky egg chair that was a pumpkin shade of orange. Cheri's spirit leans in and puts Dawn to sleep with an enchanting kiss on the mouth, and as Dawn's eyes grow heavy, Cheri's face and body became like a disco ball before cracking up into falling shards. Before Dawn could assess the situation, she had drifted into a dream sequence that was very lucid and all too real. She found herself doing things while having no control over her own body. Dawn was fingering Cheri's tight butthole, while eating her sweet vagina as if it were a fresh-baked pie that was frosted with cocaine. Cheri had Dawn's firm, young ass in her face, and was probing and cleaning her sphincter with her forked tongue.

"That's it!" Zeena shouted, cheering Cheri on. "Lick her where the sun don't shine! Hers is the secret that opens!"

Cheri coughed violently on her lover's butthole, as she grabbed Dawn's ass cheeks for dear life. Dawn felt a sharp prick on her finger, which caught her by surprise and scared the shit out of her. As Cheri violently expelled a large hair ball from her throat, Dawn slowly retracted her forefinger and middle finger from Cheri's bleached anus. As she withdrew her fingers from Cheri's treasured backdoor, she saw that her middle finger had been pierced through with a brisk fish hook. As she continued pulling out, the fishing line eventually stopped. Dawn gave it one stiff tug, and as she did, Cheri came. As Cheri went into orgasm mode, it wasn't woman juice that she ejaculated, but volcanic lava. Like a well edited television show, the scene changed within the blink of an eye. The demonic hybrid had been replaced by the Satanic princess. Dawn looked at Zeena, who was illuminating in her natural glory. The stormy priestess looked even sexier in the buff, which Dawn hadn't gotten used to and had been given too little time with. She glared at Zeena with an insatiable hunger that was unexplainable and impossible to resist.

"You look like someone I could sink my teeth into," she told Zeena, while feeling her teeth quickly grow into elongated fangs that were tough as industrial nails and sharp as straight razors.

Just as Dawn was about to rip Zeena in half and feast on her beating heart, the roles switched in a lightning instant. Dawn was somehow restrained with a dog collar, which bound and inhibited her from causing harm to herself or others. This fetish collar had taken the place of her sacred bone choker, and was a kinky strap that was designed with ruby teardrops. Along with this leather collar, she had a muzzle over her mouth that let her talk but not bite. She had been dressed in a long, black, flowing gown that had bell sleeves which were slit up the middle. The dress itself had a rather high slit, up its left side. Dawn's teeth, nails, and eyes had all returned to normal.

"Who's the alpha bitch now?" Zeena asked, proving her controlling dominance over the domesticated Cherokee. Though Dawn wasn't in a cage or on a leash, it was clear that Zeena had a power over her that she couldn't escape.

Then, out of nowhere, Dawn saw Reuben. He looked much different on the exterior, but she immediately recognized his gentle soul. He may have changed on the surface, but this didn't change what they mean to each other. The tears came rushing out, as if her ducts had become waterfalls. She had so much she wanted to say to him, but didn't know where or how to begin and couldn't bring herself to form the right words. All she could say was the word, "Daddy."

This nightmare sequence changed scenery a third time, and her lost love had tragically disappeared as quickly as he had arrived. As Cheri's health is refreshed and restored, Dawn is weakened and fatigued by their otherwise enjoyable sexual encounter. Dawn staggers and stumbles onto her feet, and slowly makes her way out of the seedy hotel room. She attempts to get some fresh air, but it's cold outside and she finds herself vulnerable to the Winter weather, which she is normally resilient towards. Finding the bitterness outdoors to be worse than the ice queen on the bed, she turns around and makes her way back inside. Her nude, Cambion lover is sitting up against the headboard with her legs spread eagle, her welcoming arms outstretched, and her eyes pleased with herself.

"Come back to Mummy," she commanded Dawn, who was beginning to feel considerably dizzy and unbalanced.

Dawn's vision began to blur, as she tried to cautiously walk back to the bed. She almost made it, coming only feet away, when she collapsed on the floor. The fatigue was just too strong, and her eyesight too clouded. Cheri let out a demonic cackle, as she threw her head back and howled. She then looked the Cherokee werewolf in the eyes, and Dawn watched in horror as Cheri's blue eyes and pink hair both turned to flame.

The atmosphere shifted again, this time to a desert environment. Dawn discovered herself lying in a tub, across from an oversized television that had a strange clarity to the picture and a futuristic flat screen. The television wasn't plugged in to anything, as she was in the middle of nowhere. Cheri was behind and underneath her in the bathtub, washing her body with a bar of soap. She fondled, groped, and fingered her American Indian playmate, while Dawn nuzzled her head against her attentive owner. Merv Griffin was announcing the lottery winner on the TV, while Dawn confided in Cheri about her innermost torment from losing Reuben. Dawn and Cheri magically switch positions, and now Dawn is holding Cheri in her loving arms. Dawn watches as the very composition of the tub becomes connecting seashells. The water in the tub becomes salty, and the two women can feel the energy vibrations as if they were laying on the beach and being hit by the waves.

Visions of Shawnee braves and Muskogee scouts materialized around the tub, as if having teleported there straight from the reservation. Cheri lays her head on Dawn's chest, just before Dawn comes out of her nightmare. When Dawn awakes, she is breathless, weakened, and struck with a mind-blowing migraine, as if she had just finished climbing the Alps in subzero temperature and then violently banged her head against a brick wall.

"Good and evil are subjective, and open to one's interpretation," Zeena told her. Though Dawn was awake now, she could still hear Zeena's gentle, but well-spoken, voice. She could also see a faint red cross floating in mid-air, which was distinguishably of Celtic design and appeared to be where Zeena's voice was coming from.

"A new age is coming, where Christianity will have outlived its welcome and the Bible will be looked at as fiction," Nikolas's voice added, which was clearly less soft, but equally as articulate and seemingly intelligent.

Dawn didn't know if it was her dysfunctional history, her being damaged goods, or her being a werewolf, but figured she must be more unhinged than she had initially thought, if she could hear voices from people who weren't physically there. Then again, this was no weirder than her seeing visions of her dead mother, imploring her to not kill. The difference was that neither Zeena or Nikolas were deceased, unlike Linda. Dawn quickly reaches up to feel her neck, to make sure that she's wearing her stolen bone choker that had grown to become such a part of her. She sighed in relief, to feel it still there and to understand that what she had just suffered was merely a dream, though an incredibly evocative and eloquent one.

It is here that Dawn meets Richard, as he's the one she finds at her side, who had been trying to shake her out of her nightmare. He had shown up an hour ago, arriving in a candy apple red 1974 *Pontiac Trans Am*. Richard was very charming and seemed harmless, even though he was clearly a bit odd. He was 18-years-old and dressed all in black. His hair was long, black, and greasy, but that didn't appear to take away from his charisma. He knew how to swoon women, regardless of their age, and was well versed in what they wanted to hear. Dawn was looking for a reason to convince herself that she wasn't a lesbian, still uncomfortable with her undying feelings for Cheri. She was also scanning for a way to get back at Cheri for playing her. Dawn had scarlet fever again, with Cheri, like she had with Reuben, and she couldn't deny it without lying to herself. Though they hadn't properly been introduced, and he hadn't offered his name, Dawn felt strangely compelled to choose Richard to confide her darkest secrets. They began to chat as if they had known each other for years, and as Dawn opened up to him, a couple of the other girls sat in front of the TV and played *Atari 2600* games.

Mathias sees this intimate interaction between Richard and Dawn, and out of sheer jealously, retires outside to the garden, disrobes, and makes snow angels in the soft dirt, as the failed alchemist lays flat on his back and drools over himself. His chest tattoo faces the morning sun, a symbol known as the *Udjat* (or *all seeing eye*), which is an eye with a diamond-shaped tear directly underneath it. Joy, on the other hand, politely bows out of the party and silently slips away upstairs. Isolating herself in his private bathroom, which was part of Mathias's master bedroom and off limits to those without explicit permission, she locks the door behind her. This hidden and exclusive bathroom is colored in harvest gold, burnt orange, and avocado. There are flickering lights framed around the mirror's border, which she uses for a moment to indulge in her vanity.

Joy fiddles with her left nipple, which is tattooed with a triangle that hung underneath, with her areola and nipple both outlined and traced in circles. She was naked now and knelt before his toilet, with the lid and seat both raised. She mixed together one teaspoon each of these essential oils, in the toilet water: rose, almond, jojoba, musk, and ambergris. She then poured two tablespoons of Venus oil into the porcelain cauldron, adding it to the recipe. Behind the toilet, sitting atop the tank, was a glass jar that contained a preserved lamb's heart. Joy lit a red candle, which waited for her on the corner of his bathtub. The tub was partially filled with *Fisher-Price* Little People, which he sometimes got off on watching his girls play with. This was a candle that she had earlier saturated with Jasmine oil, by stroking it up and down like it was a dildo. The red candle smelled of cinnamon, but was comprised of a mixture of baby fat, blood, and wax. She had carefully carved her name and Dawn's name into the side of the long, vertical candle that was embossed with images of skulls.

"I call upon you, Isis, Goddess of Luna, to work with Aphrodite and Venus in blessing me with Dawn's affections."

As the oiled candle burned, Joy leaned her head over the tidy bowl, and proceeded to use both hands to thoroughly wash her face with the witchy mixture in the sewage receptacle. As she scrubbed her skin with the toilet brew, she trusted the demonically-charged potion to empower her selfish desire, expecting Lady Isis to grant her the wishes and lusts of her charcoal heart. The curvaceous Joy Zanetti then lifted the candle off the tub's edge, and pressed it up against her ample chest. She placed it back onto the flat side of the tub, and cupped her hands over the flickering blue and orange flame. As she could feel the tremendous heat singe her flesh, she meditated on what she wanted and what she asked to happen if she didn't get it.

"Gracious Isis, you are the ancient Goddess of the hunt and of Luna. You possess the power to communicate with and control the wildest of animals. I beg you to let this love spell work, but if it proves ineffective and Dawn rejects my advances, I ask that you rain down on her your mighty wrath and avenge me with her unbearable and unmitigated suffering."

She took Dawn's new flask, placed it over the bi-colored flame, and then dunked it in the tidy bowl beverage, thereby cursing it on the condition that she submit to her will or be severely penalized with brutal consequences. Joy was clueless to the fact that Mathias had already cast a similar spell for identical reasons, including shoving the opening of the flask up his filthy anus and farting on it.

"As I unleash the beast in Dawn, let her embrace the beast in me," Joy closed in privacy, before she smothered the flame by gently squeezing the wick with her delicate, yet diabolical, fingers.

As Joy extinguished the undisclosed candle, her fingertips momentarily caught on fire, as if the burning light had transferred from one to the other. The red candle was now a lavender color, which was a shade used to provoke relaxation and sedation, or to bring someone under total submission. Joy needed Dawn to loosen up, when it came to her, and she would do everything in her infernal power to make that happen. She concluded the sinister ritual by blowing three times into the silver flask to seal the curse. As she returned to the party, Dawn had just noticed that her flask had mysteriously disappeared, and was frantically searching for it as she attempted to retrace her steps. She was determined to not lose another one, and this new one was of such fine quality that it inspired and motivated her even further to hold onto it. She saw Mathias, and nervously asked him if he had seen it lying around anywhere.

"I have it," Joy said, as she creeped up behind her. "I thought I'd be nice and fill it with moonshine for you."

"Oh," Dawn said, sighing with relief, while Mathias looked perplexed. "Thank God. Thank you, Joy. I sincerely appreciate it."

"No problem, sweetie," Joy said. "It's my pleasure. I like looking after you."

As Joy turned her back and walked away, her honey brown eyes turned to yellow with red pupils, just for a brief moment. Joy grinned wickedly with self-gratification, as she took sick satisfaction from deceiving not only Dawn, but the rest of *The Golden Veil*. Nobody knew, not even Magus Mathias, that Joy was actually an Arae. She was an invoked demon who was the result of a curse that was placed by Crowley himself, posthumous, for malevolent purposes. She was never intended to remain on earth after serving the duty of her summoning, but was able to find a loophole in the hex. As long as she remained linked with those who worshipped Aleister Crowley, she could escape having to go back to the bottomless pits of Hell. The eyes are truly the windows to the soul, and nobody had thought enough to look into Joy's, which only further amused her.

"This is almost too easy," Joy said softly to herself, as she relished in the pathetic fact that her fellow Thelemites, as well as Dawn, were all completely ignorant of the incarnate evil that surrounded them…and that would ultimately be there demise.

She relished in the distinct lack of intuition, which engulfed and infected the coven like a plague. Lucifer has cruel intentions, and Joy was certainly no different. She was as much of a fraud and as starved for malice, as the Devil herself. Dawn would learn to bow to her and succumb to her every demand, or pay the price with her eternal soul. When Mathias had earlier blighted the cherished item with his own version and personalization, he pressed it up against his venomous heart while he involuntarily rocked back and forth, as if on the razor's edge of insanity.

"Horned god, Osiris," Mathias recalled saying aloud to himself, but in a volume that only he could hear, "Inspiration to my mentor, Aleister Crowley, the founder of sorcery and alchemy, show me what is unseen. Grant me the knowledge of the fallen angels, and disclose to me the secrets of the Tree of Life. Enlighten me that which God denies and begrudges man. Guide me on how to win Dawn's submission and break her in, so that I don't have to unleash the beast within me and rip her to fucking shreds."

This had been Mathias's Satanic prayer, which preceded Joy's more elaborate curse. They both craved Dawn's succulent body, and neither would stop their tireless pursuit until Dawn dropped her guard and surrendered to their will and wile. Meanwhile, a third party continues to fight for Dawn's attention, who seemed to be having a much easier time achieving that and beating this challenge.

"I love it how Christians condemn pornography, when sex is only celebrating God's creation. God made our bodies desirable. God gave us our primal lusts and needs. Yet, we're supposed to be ashamed of sex and judge others for doing what they were designed to do?" Richard preached. "That just makes me sick. The Christian hypocrisy, in this country, is appalling to me. If I'm a monster, it's only because God made me that way. Oh, wait...that's right, God never makes mistakes."

Dawn talked about her sour experience with orthodox Christianity, as she bears witness to college-type hazing and sexual harassment. The girls in the coven were being treated like toys, and the compound felt more like a brothel. As she tried to listen to what Richard was saying, it disturbed her to watch these girls be so violated and humiliated. Men and women alike casually bent these girls over or pushed their heads down, demanding that they please them in whatever way they wished, without either asking for consent or permission, and with no exchange of monetary payment. There was nothing off limits. Some of *The Golden Veil* girls were literally living up to their coven's name, as they swallowed the piss from different dicks and cunts, gulping it down as if it was strawberry wine.

"John Wayne Gacy was a Christian," Richard educated. "He read the 23rd Psalm to his victims, before brutally sacrificing them."

"Do you think someone who kills is evil?" Dawn inquired curiously, while shaking her head in disgust, rapidly and strenuously blinking her eyes, and trying to force herself to focus and concentrate on her private conversation.

"We are all evil, in one form or another. Serial killers do on a small scale what governments do on a large one. They are a product of the times, and these are bloodthirsty times. Even psychopaths have emotions if you dig deep enough, but then again…maybe they don't. People, this day and age, are brainwashed and programmed like a computer, and being nothing more than puppets. This nation, this country, is founded in violence. Violent delights tend to have violent ends. Madness is something rare in individuals, but in groups it is something ruling and revered. Killing is killing, whether done for duty, profit, or fun. Men murder themselves into this democracy. America is the land of opportunity for those who are truly sinister, while doing its best to kill off those who try their hardest to live right. Our country rewards its murderers, as long as they are the ones in position of power or authority."

"If I tell you something, will you give me your solemn word that it will stay between us, and only us?" Dawn asked for his pledge of confidence, as she continued taking healthy sips from her large, silver flask.

"Yes, of course," Richard agreed, seeing the seriousness on her face. He could tell that something was eating at her and didn't want to add to her distress.

"I'm scared of Mathias. I think he may be a Satanist," Dawn trusted, as she held her head, feeling dizzy and starting to lose her balance. She chocked it up as being symptomatic of dealing with stress and anxiety, not even considering the possibility that she could have been sabotaged or cursed. Her hypocrisy was apparent even to her, as it hadn't bothered her in the slightest that Zeena had identified herself as an admitted and prideful Devil worshipper. Mathias, on the other hand, was an entirely different story and made her feel an entirely different way.

The twisted Crowleyan leader was watching from a distance, grinning from ear to ear, dressed like a European marquis. He wore a *Menat* amulet, which is believed to preserve in the dead the desire and ability to engage in sexual activities. The scarab-shaped medallion has phallic characteristics, and is comprised of bronze and copper. Hanging around his neck, the talisman is suspended over his back so that it could exert its aphrodisiac qualities directly on the spinal column.

"There are different sects of Satanism," Richard said, smiling. "I can tell you a little bit about Satanism. It is undefiled wisdom instead of hypocritical self-deceit. It is power without charity. The perfect world most people seek shall never come to pass, and it's going to get worse. The great itbox of our lives is when we gain the courage to re-baptize our evil qualities as our best qualities. Black-robed pagans would come to congregate at Stonehenge, leaving the Judeo-Christian archetype to advocate Satanism. They did this because they got sick and tired of seeing too many Christians who weren't Christians, and resented God for blessing and saving only discriminately, helping those under the middle finger of favoritism. Satanism is the ultimate rebellion against God's chuckling, and the freedom from his savagery."

"I think he wants me. I think Mathias wants me in the worst way," Dawn expressed in a volume for his ears only, as a concise cry for help, hoping that Richard might rescue her from her stalker's unwanted advances.

"I wouldn't worry too much about it," Richard responded, as the trippy Dawn dropped to the floor, collapsing and crashing in coercion. "I've known that

Grand Poobah for years. Trust me, he's all bark and no bite," he said grinning, as he looked down on the irresistibly appetizing, and now helplessly vulnerable, sexpot whom he was all too eager to claim as his own...at least for the night.

Dawn has another nightmare, under her defunct duress, where she dreams of 17th century France. It's the year of our Lord, 1630, where 30,000 people were being vindictively interrogated for allegedly being werewolves. Much like the Salem Witch Trials 62 years later, these accused were regular folks, viciously labeled with false charges that were completely unfounded. These were peasants and tailors, and common, ordinary citizens, who paid dearly for the hysteria at that time. There were countless testimonies from those who claimed to have caught the chastised in compromising situations, like being covered in blood or seen with having fur from head to toe. This caused mass paranoia, which was confused for being a threatening epidemic. While crowds of self-righteous, pious Christians gathered around to cheer and applaud the executions, the law enforcers slaughtered these alleged heretics by driving blades through their hearts that were made of mercury (also known as *quicksilver*). This appalling exhibit of so-called justice would be only one of innumerable examples of *Christians* acting out in behavior that was the antithesis of, and inconsistent with, what the Bible actually teaches.

Dawn awoke the following morning, covered in minor cuts and moderate bruises, to find Richard vainly looking at himself in the mirror. She found herself in Mathias's gigantic master bedroom, which was predominately green. Dawn immediately regretted the previous night of casual (and evidently rough) sex with Richard. There were steel handcuffs on the nightstand and blood stains on the sheets under her ass, which was incredibly sore. She had a horrendous, pulsating migraine from the hangover she had partially earned. Richard stood there, admiring his own reflection and gloating about his looks, while she held her agonized head in her trembling hands. He had drawn an inverted pentagram on the back of his left hand and in the center of his forehead, using a tube of black *Cover Girl* lipstick. She looked at him, both from behind and through the mirror's eyes. She saw blood on his penis, that she could only assume was hers. She also noticed a large hunting knife laying on the dresser in front of him, which had blood both on the handle and on the blade. She couldn't remember any details from the night they shared, but based on the way she felt and how things appeared, she had put it together that whatever happened must have been really bad.

"God, I'm so sexy," the narcissist said aloud to himself, showing his egocentric side. "I should really be on TV. I want to be on TV." There were traces of LSD on the table in front of the sofa. Dawn had vaguely remembered her twilight of meaningless sex with him, but knew nothing else about this human parasite and had no idea what he actually was.

"I'm sorry," she apologized softly, still reeling from her splitting headache. "What's your name?"

"Richard," he answered with shameless pride, as he grinned from ear to ear. "Richard Ramirez."

Dawn finds herself suddenly overcome with fear, and gets the strong sense that she had made a horrible mistake. Before she could come up with an excuse to leave the room and flee from the compound, Richard had telepathically read her mind.

"Don't even think about it," he told her. "You're not going anywhere, bitch. Well…at least not where you think."

Dawn felt her heart pound practically out of her chest, as her teeth and nails grew long and jagged. Her beautiful blue eyes turned black, and her naked flesh became durable and much hairier; but, as usual, only she could see these changes. She sprung to her hands and knees, and was about to leap off the bed and violently pounce on him, when a dark specter appeared behind Richard's back to protect him. This shadowy wraith was black as pitch, had gaping holes for eyes, and wore vintage, tethered threads. It hovered in the air while showing Dawn its own claws, which were much more threatening and terrifying than hers. The homicidal Cherokee was frozen in petrifying fear and couldn't move or shift. Dawn growled at the malignant specter, trying to intimidate it by showing her teeth and giving the facade of being fierce, but her commendable attempts were futile. Linda's ghost had also failed to show up, which was a sign to Dawn that she couldn't kill Ramirez if she wanted to. As Dawn gazed at the heinous specter, and looked into its empty eyes, it made her do some soul searching. She had fancied herself as an honorable vigilante, but as she reflected on her growing bloodlust and relentless warpath, she wondered if she was as much of a monster as this evil specter was, which internally brought her terror like she had never known.

"Legitimate Satanists view these sociopaths as being the failures of Satanism," Nikolas said, as she heard his voice again, even though he and Zeena were miles away and nowhere to be found. "Self-styled Satanists are despised not dignified. They're perpetual losers or what we call pseudo-Satanists. We frown upon such experimenting enthusiasts, dabblers, and spectating posers. Those who commit atrocities in Satan's name, are either unhinged, or *radical* psychos who have nothing to do with legitimate Satanic philosophy."

"God, help me," Dawn begged out loud, as she feared not just for her life, but for her very soul.

"Oh, my dear Dawn," Richard said, smiling in amusement, "God doesn't care about you. Matthew 10:34 and 35 tell us that God is not a god of peace but a god of war, who longs to turn loved ones against each other. That's why your minister father raped you. That's why God took Reuben away, took Donnie away, and why he split you and Cheri apart. This is the *real* Lord thy God. He couldn't care less about you, little girl, but in fact takes pleasure in your pain and suffering."

The broken Cherokee deeply regretted ever running away from Cheri. Though she still was unable to forgive her for how she had initially used her, she realized that Cheri wasn't the monster that she believed herself to be. Cheri loved her, and Dawn knew that to be true, which was precisely why she was now missing her so desperately. If Cheri had been there, she could probably help Dawn fight fire with fire, but being delivered from Richard and his demon was far less important to her than just being with Cheri. She just wanted to be back in the pink Cambion's arms again, but it was too late. Dawn had made her bed, and now had to sleep in it. She was trapped, now paying the consequences for her actions and reaping the whirlwind of her mistakes. Dawn also hurt over abandoning Wolf, who had been the best friend she ever had. She loved him dearly and they both knew each other to be kindred spirits. By leaving him, she left a big part of herself. She worried about him now, and only hoped that Cheri was taking care of him on her behalf. Dawn was a renegade with a cause, but had her impetuous behavior been worth her own misery and now the suffering of those she loved? She hadn't expected to ever love again, after losing her precious Reuben, but now her angry rebellion towards God had hurt two souls whom she adored and would gladly die for.

"Your dyke friend can't save you either," Richard confirmed, once again proving that he could telepathically read her thoughts, whether she wanted him to or not. "You and I, baby…we're going on a little trip, which isn't open for debate or discussion, so…you might as well relax and enjoy the ride, like you did last night," he said, grinning like a wild hyena, pleased with himself and his swooning and wooing talents.

Dawn was on the middle bed, and as her eyes wandered around the enormous room, she spotted the shrine, which frightened her far more than Richard's specter. The altar was moderate, but considerably creepy. It was basically a wooden platform, covered with a black silk tablecloth to cushion and protect what laid atop. There was a crimson idol of Baphomet in the center, surrounded by a skull mala, a stained-glass thunderbolt, a green baboon fetish, a lizard totem, a crystal ball with a deon inside, a metal thunderbolt, and a three-dimensional chaosphere in the bottom right hand corner. Then, in the middle of it all, was a framed photograph of Dawn.

She thought back when she had asked Cheri if they could have their picture taken together, and Cheri declined. As stunning a woman as Cheri was, her self-image was low and she wasn't thrilled with, or fond of, the idea of having photographic mementos or souvenirs of what she perceived to be her ugliness. Dawn still couldn't budge a muscle, as she posed like a gargoyle, scrutinizing the executioner in progress. Suddenly, Joy's curse kicked in full gear, and Dawn became infected with an infirmity that took all the fight out of her. She slowly began to fade, as her eyes grew heavy, her heart slowed, and she fell reluctantly into the pitch darkness.

SEPTEMBER 7, 1968
SATURDAY
RED MOON

Before the 1968 Miss America Pageant, most Americans had never heard of the women's liberation movement. But on this day in history, a protest outside the *Miss America Pageant,* at the Atlantic City Convention Center, drew the nation's eye. As millions of viewers tuned in to watch the pageant, they witnessed nearly 400 women carrying signs reading, *No More Beauty Standards* and *Welcome to the Cattle Auction*, as they decried the concept of beauty contests.

At the center of this commotion was the *Freedom Can*, a trash receptacle into which women threw high heels, girdles, dish detergent, curlers, *Playboy* magazines, and bras, calling them *instruments of female torture*. Although these protesters had intended to burn the items, they were unsuccessful in obtaining a fire permit. In the end, no bras ever went up in flames. This, however, didn't stop the protesters from earning a nickname that would stick well into the 1970s and beyond: *bra burners*. This term was coined by the reporters covering the women's liberation protest, who compared their movement to anti-war protesters who publicly burned draft cards and flags. These women, as with most civil rights demonstrators, were beaten mercilessly by the police and treated even worse by the traditionally corrupt court system. Linda was among these protesters, and was an avid activist for women's liberation, which was a bit hypocritical, considering how easy it was for her to spread her legs for any man who showed interest.

Linda relished in remembering how Dawn had been born under a full moon…a night not unlike this night. Those who had escaped the police abuse and apprehension, were celebrating now underneath the stars, drinking, getting stoned, and partying with anyone regardless of consent. The full moon is shining its silver beams upon the shadows of the open field, where the orgy is taking place. Linda is grasping a silver coin in her left hand, as if for dear life, while her seminary boyfriend…along with select family members and friends…take turns mercilessly raping her in their preferred holes. *The Doors* hit song, *Back Door Man*, is playing over the radio. Mingan Moon is wearing a lizard-skin, buttoned-down shirt that he had lifted from a luxurious retail outlet.

JANUARY 13, 1979
BIRCH MOON

As Cheri rolls on down the highway, in her blue 1975 *Dodge Ram* Van 150, the Little River Band song, *Lady*, plays over the automotive stereo. A full moon lights the night sky above, as if there to guide their path. Wolf is sitting there, behind and beside Cheri's seat, keeping her company and making sure she stays alert. He looks sad, as if pessimistic about the outcome of their determined journey. Cheri tries to think positive, as they unknowingly drive directly into the age of iniquity. Cheri brings her finger up to her lips, that has the moonstone ring, and places the crystal in her mouth. As she sucks on it, like it was a piece of hard candy, she sees the future and it terrifies her.

"Don't you worry, buddy," Cheri tells Wolf, not blind to the hopelessness on his face. "We'll find her. I won't give up until we do."

Cheri thinks about her identical twin sister who died three days after her birth, who was going to be named *Bovina*. She felt as if she had a new sister now, in Dawn, and was dead set on not letting her go…or down. She's wearing a distressed jean jacket, with a white jockbra underneath. The Captain & Tennille song, *Love Will*

Keep Us Together, starts playing over the radio airwaves, further encouraging Cheri to not surrender hope, in spite of the grim odds of them finding a happy ending.

***

That next morning, back in Silver Spring, MD, at the Nazarene church, the despicable yet popular Rev. Mingan Moon is giving one of his usual charismatic sermons. He tries his best to rush through his prepared message, as he has plans that afternoon to take his floozy secretary to the *Crystal Grottoes Caverns* in Boonsboro, hoping to get lost in the dark cave and show her his own stalagmite.

"In Native American mythology, the man on the moon wanted to lay with young Indian woman. She climbed tall tree to speak with him about this. She agreed to comply to his wishes, if he would marry her and refuse to shine on any other person. He laughed at her unreasonable proposition. She jumps on his chest, therefore causing the dark pattern we now see on the moon," the two-faced preacher shared, expressing his disgust with how willful, ungrateful, and spiteful women are.

Back at Mathias's Midland compound, Agent Shelling had arrived at the scene and now stood amidst what looked to have been a bloodbath. All of the coven members are brutally butchered, except for Emily 'Jezebel' Bryant, who is shaken and hysterical. She's putting on a performance of a lifetime, as she falsely testifies that Dawn Moon had been the one to senselessly slaughter her friends. The only ones who aren't accounted for, from *The Golden Veil* grotto, are Mathias and Joy, but Emily made sure to not mention them. The high priestess had disposed of her peers, with Mathias's blessing, with the intention of slandering and punishing Dawn for rejecting their advances. These were the same girls who would have gladly given their lives for Mathias, and who had offered their bodies to him daily (whether he commanded them to or not), yet they clearly meant nothing to him. Joy, of course, couldn't have been more pleased to have effectively exterminated the competition, as she now had Mathias's undivided attention. Joy thrived on being his second in command, but he had no idea that he meant as little to her as the the other girls had meant to him.

"You have to protect me!" Emily cried out, trying to distract the Federal Agent from analyzing why she had been spared, when she was evidently no ally of Dawn's. "She might come back for me! I can't stay here! Please...help me!" Though Emily acted convincing in her dire straits, Agent Shelling did observe that her voice seemed awfully stable, when others in her shoes would have been more flustered and incoherent.

Trying to calm her down and get her to compose herself, he instructed her what not to do if she did see the primary suspect again.

"If Dawn does return here, whatever you do...do not engage," he said, as his eyes revealed that he couldn't really give a shit about this survivor, who strangely had no blood on her and was completely untouched.

He briefly considered using Emily as a way to lure Dawn out, but something told him that this wasn't somebody whom Dawn cared to see again. He asked her question after question, hoping for a little more insight on Dawn, but her answers felt as if they were a memorized script. Agent Shelling knew that this scenario didn't feel right, but couldn't outright accuse Emily of impeding or obfuscating to impair his case. She demanded to be put into protective custody, expressing interest in Witness Relocation, but there were no signs that she had been in any danger, even if Dawn had been the assassin. He also knew something was amiss when she tried to convince him that Dawn was armed, and had shot and stabbed everyone, when neither was part of Dawn's M.O.

Agent Shelling finally had the local police escort Emily to the station for further questioning. After rigorous inspection of the bodies, he noticed that none of them shared any similarities to Dawn's previous victims. He also noticed that there was no animal hair anywhere, which was always a factor of Dawn's slayings. Though there was no evidence to suggest that Dawn had any part in these particular murders, he chose to keep this knowledge to himself and let the department believe that Dawn was the culprit. Agent Shelling was so hung up on making her pay for William, that he didn't care about the extent of her guilt. As far as he was concerned, she was dangerous, and he would continue his pursuit until she joined William six feet under.

EPILOGUE

Meanwhile, Heather Campbell was further rewarded, abundantly, for being a sadistic sociopath. Not only did Heather win the state lottery, but she suddenly inherited a million dollars after her father mysteriously died of pneumonia the day after he was awarded a settlement for medical malpractice. "Praise Jesus!" Heather insincerely exclaimed, as she literally laughed all the way to the bank, proving that the wicked are blessed while the good are forsaken. This, of course, begged the question if God was a respecter of persons, as he seemed to favor and reward the maliciously sadistic.

It's Monday, February 26, 1979. Cheri stopped at a mystical shoppe, to get some fresh air and stretch her legs. There is a solar eclipse tonight, and Cheri and Wolf both needed a short break from their pilgrimage of rescue. As she browsed through the different candles, incense sticks, and crystals, she came across a medallion that really caught her eye and immediately captured her interest. This amulet is of a sphere sitting atop a horizontal block. She picked it up and held it securely in her hand. As she did this, the medallion glowed and sparkled.

"That's the *Shen*," the shopkeeper educated her, watching her admire the magical relic. "It's a symbol of eternity and the all-embracing power of the sun god, *Ra*." Cheri just responded with a blank glance, signaling to the Wichita-raised practitioner that his comment had left her dazed and confused. The arcane vendor just smiled, and continued to further explain and potentially enlighten. "The sun represents a lot of different things," the esoteric merchant went on, "like prosperity, hope, health, and fame. The *Shen*, however, especially symbolizes the prolonging of human life."

"Are you saying that wearing this around my neck will make me live forever?" Cheri inquired, having doubts about this madman's legitimacy and credibility.

"Well...no...but, it does have the power to maintain and sustain your youth. You will find that you will age much slower, if at all," he told Cheri, making outrageous claims that somehow weren't outside of Cheri's open mind.

Cheri and Wolf rolled on down the highway in her groovy van, with the sun-god medallion now tied to and hanging from the rearview mirror, as if it were fuzzy dice or a cheap air freshener. She would have lassoed it around her neck, but she had a hard time swallowing the retailer's incredible pitch. Cheri, however, was secretly terrified of her own mortality, as she knew where she was destined to go when death decided to knock at her door. Being half succubus didn't allow a whole lot of room for hope, so the afterlife traumatized her whenever she let her mind dwell on it for too long. Though she realized she would eventually have to face her fear, and accept her fate that she couldn't change, it didn't alter her need to live, breathe, and...love. She needed to rectify her sins and reconcile with Dawn, as she was genuinely repentant of her selfish deeds. She had hurt the one she loved, and nothing was going to stop her from making things right while she still could.

The hours passed like a brief breeze, night had fallen once again, and the pink-haired Cambion began to feel her eyelids get uncontrollably heavy. She fought her exhaustion for awhile, but inevitably could no longer resist. Wolf would have kept her awake and alert, but he had dosed off into his own wonderland. As Cheri began to cave to slumber's calming invite, she saw a shadowy figure in the middle of her lane. Fear perked her up as she instinctively and immediately attempted to swerve around the standing silhouette. This rash motion was reckless and done so in panic, not prevention. The van came close to tipping over on its left side, but two husky, wolf-like shadows appeared out of nowhere, leapt up, and used the force of their bodies to knock the van back on all four wheels. Before she knew it, Cheri had driven right through the dark figure, and as she did, the van vibrated as if it had been electrified. The van had come to a dead stop, and not from the brake being applied. For a fleeting moment, which felt like much longer, Cheri and Wolf found themselves in a charcoal cloud of mist. A female form appeared before them, who was solid black, except for her bright opaque eyes. She told Cheri, through telepathy, that her name was Hazel. She wore rabbit's feet for earrings, which Cheri only saw in silhouette…like the rest of the mysterious figure.

"Turn back," Hazel warned her, in a voice which was even creepier than her shady appearance. "This won't end well for you, and you can't save her."

Cheri didn't know how to respond, so she didn't. After a few moments of silence, Hazel faded away into nothingness, and the engine started again…all on its own. Cheri refused to be dissuaded or discouraged, as she had her mind set on ensuring that she and Dawn would have more than just a season in the sun.

ABOUT THE AUTHOR

Nicholas was bullied throughout school, nicknamed *Frankenstein* for his oversized head. He would later come to love the Horror genre. After a harrowing divorce in November 2013 (the 5th anniversary of losing his beloved daughter and her selfish mother, Andrea), to his 2nd pseudo-wife whom he'd discover to be a pathological liar, proud prostitute, and sadistic identity thief, Nicholas would fall apart and come dangerously close to death. He'd suffer panic attacks and suicidal thoughts, while watching his sweet daughter endure night terrors, all over the 27-year-old monster that he regretfully entrusted their vulnerable hearts. Heather certainly wouldn't be the first to take joy from crucifying him, but would be the most atrocious sociopath he'd ever have the misfortune of knowing. This callous betrayal would crush his spirit, but also liberate his creativity. Nick's heart may be forever fractured, but his imagination is infinite and incomparable. Erica (his celestial fiancé) and Harley (his precious daughter) keep him going. He strives to make a name for himself as an actor and a writer, while battling several health concerns, including a weak aortic valve, failing vision, and multiple malfunctioning organs.

Also by Nicholas Knight: